CHARMING FIONA

A SEDUCTIVE ROMANCE

JESSICA PRINCE

CIVIL CORRUPTION SERIES

Corrupt

Defile (Declan and Tatum's story – coming 2018)

GIRL TALK SERIES:

Seducing Lola

Tempting Sophia

Enticing Daphne

Charming Fiona

STANDALONE TITLES:

Chance Encounters

Nightmares from Within

DEADLY LOVE SERIES:

Destructive

Addictive

CO-WRITTEN BOOKS:

Hustler – with Meghan Quinn

PROLOGUE

FIONA

AS CHILDREN we were taught that the sky was the limit, that when we reached adulthood we could become whatever we wanted. For a long time I'd taken that far too literally, first deciding that I wanted to be a Barbie doll, then a princess, then a mermaid—*that one's on you, Ariel.*

When I finally got over the heartbreak of discovering that Disney princesses didn't actually exist in real life, I decided I wanted to be the first woman president or an astronaut. That phase hadn't lasted long.

When I reached my teenage years, my father began grooming me to take over the family business. After all, I was Calvin and Evelyn Prentice's only child. So it came without saying that I'd one day carry on the legacy that had started as nothing more than a small, family-run department store on the West Coast and eventually grew into a worldwide fashion empire thanks to my father, and his father before him, and so on and so forth.

Most teenage girls would have dreamed of working in the high-end fashion industry, reveling in all the perks, the haute couture. But I wasn't one of those girls. I didn't dream of running an empire. I didn't care about notoriety or fame or any of that stuff.

I didn't care about being the next big "it" name or who walked down the red carpet in one of our designs.

Truth was, I hadn't earned any of that. It had just been handed down to me as the next Prentice generation. No, what I wanted more than anything in the world was to be a wonderful wife and mother. Yes, I was aware that my ambitions set feminism back by decades, but I didn't give a shit. I wanted a family. I'd grown up watching my father dote on my mother like she was the only woman on the planet. They kissed, they touched, they didn't care where they were or who saw their sometimes sickening—especially to a school-aged girl—displays of affection.

Most days my dad could barely keep his hands off her. And I was sure that, had my mom been able to, our house would have been *full* of children.

Unfortunately her body just wasn't built to carry a baby. Her pregnancy with me was difficult enough, and after nine months of living in constant fear for his wife's well-being, my father had decided that one was more than enough.

When I finally came into the world, I got all that adoration and love showered on me as well, so it had been ingrained in me from day one to find a man who treated me like I walked on water, and to hold on tight.

Because of that, I'd grown up with a somewhat inflated sense of romance. Meaning I threw myself into every single relationship I ever entered and had my heart crushed when they eventually came to an end.

But the absolute worst heartbreak I'd ever encountered had come at the hands of a man I'd grown up with. A man whom I'd idolized and placed on a pedestal for as long as I could remember.

Grayson Lockhart was absolutely *everything* a woman could want. He was kind and sweet, he was driven in success, smart, funny, and tying all of that up with a shiny, perfect bow was the fact that he looked like a Greek god.

The man was hot. I was talking take-your-breath-away, drench-your-panties *hot*. He could give you a mini-orgasm just by walking into a room and smiling.

And he'd been all mine.

For a time.

When our relationship ended, I'd been devastated. I threw myself into work, eventually jetting off to Prentice Fashion's Paris headquarters. I just couldn't take seeing him with other women. And since our families were such close friends, it felt like every exploit since our breakup was being shoved down my throat.

It wasn't until years later when I'd finally managed to mend my broken heart that I realized Grayson was never supposed to be my everything.

No, that title belonged to the one boy who'd been a central figure in my life practically since day one. He was the one who held me when I cried, who I shared my deepest and darkest fears with, who knew each and every one of my hopes and dreams.

He had once been my everything, and I'd been too stupid to realize it, even though it had been right in front of my face all my life.

I'd been taught that I could be anything, do anything, that true, unflinching love really did exist.

But what I *hadn't* been taught was that it didn't wait forever.

Eventually true love got tired of sitting around, waiting for you to get your head out of your ass and realize you'd picked the wrong brother.

And that was exactly what had happened to me, because by the time I realized that Deacon Lockhart was the love of my life, it was too late.

And I had no one to blame but myself.

CHAPTER ONE

DEACON

"I JUST DON'T UNDERSTAND why they don't like me," Leah went on... and on, and on. "I mean, we've been together for three months now and they *still* treat me like I don't belong. What have I ever done to any of them?"

Fuck me, this was a mistake.

The entire car ride to Caleb and Daphne's place had been one long bitchfest about my friends and how they still hadn't accepted my girlfriend. If I was being completely honest, I was getting pretty fucking tired of listening to it.

"Christ, Leah, if my friends make you so damn miserable, then why'd you insist on coming today, huh?"

She crossed her arms and pouted at my windshield. We were still too early in our relationship for me to have decided if this was something that was going to last, or if it was just a way for me to get my feet wet in an attempt to move on from Fiona.

I'd spent way too fucking long pining for a woman who'd never be mine, and it was time get on with my life. Sure, there had been plenty of other women over the years, but not for any other reason than getting off when the need arose. It was long past time to let Fee go completely and try to build something with someone else.

I couldn't say for sure that Leah was going to be the one, but after my older brother Grayson got married and knocked up his wife, Lola, I started to feel like something serious was missing from my life. I wasn't necessarily ready to settle down and have my woman pop out a handful of kids, but if I had any hopes of that being in my future, I needed to get my head out of my ass and stop clinging to something that was never going to happen.

It was what it was. Fiona was a friend. That was all she was ever going to see me as, just a guy she grew up with. She'd said as much herself that terrible fucking night that was still burned into my brain after all this time.

I let out a slow, calming breath as I took the last step onto the porch. I wasn't sure what came over me but when I left my bar, The Black Sheep, I drove straight to Fiona's house, determined that tonight was the night.

Maybe it was because my brother had his shit together and was settling down with Lola. Maybe it was because I was watching Dominic and Caleb jump through hoops, trying to get their women's attention. I felt like everyone was attempting to move on with their lives but me. I was being left in the dust.

"Deacon?" Christ, she was beautiful, even with the confusion marring her face when she opened the front door. "Is everything okay? It's really late."

I raked a hand through my hair in agitation. I hadn't thought about the time or the fact that she'd worry with me showing up at her door in the middle of the night. I was an asshole. "Yeah, shit. Yes. Sorry. Everything's fine. I didn't realize how late it was."

Her head tilted to the side as her forehead wrinkled. "But didn't you just come from closing the bar?"

Son of a bitch. I was fucking this all to hell. "Yeah. Right. Shit. I'm screwing this up."

"Hey." Fiona stepped across the threshold onto the porch, reaching out to place a calming hand on my forearm. The feel of her palm against my skin sent electric shock waves through my system. That was all it ever took with her, just a simple touch or look and I was completely undone. "It's okay," she continued in a soothing tone. "Just tell me what's going on. I want to help."

Christ, she was killing me. "I should've acted sooner," I stated, lost in her eyes. "Fuck, I should've told Grayson the truth. He wouldn't have betrayed me like that if I'd just told him the fucking truth. Then all these years wouldn't have been wasted."

I wasn't making any sense. I knew that, but I couldn't seem to bring myself to elaborate. My brain was locked on one singular task, making it impossible to concentrate on anything but my desperate need for her.

"Deac, honey. You're starting to worry me. You aren't making any sense. What should you have told Grayson?"

I knew I should answer, that it was the logical thing to do considering I wasn't making a damn bit of sense. But I wasn't thinking, so I let instinct take over and did the one thing I'd been wanting to do most of my life.

Grabbing the back of her neck, I yanked her body into mine, winding my other arm around her waist as I crashed my lips to hers. She froze stiff for several seconds, like she was unsure what was happening. However, the instant my tongue snaked out and ran across her full bottom lip, she groaned, falling deeper into me as her mouth opened in an invitation.

She tasted sweet, like cherries and that red wine she was such a fan of. I'd kept it stocked in my bar just for her, even though we'd spent the past several years distant from each other. I'd only gotten her back recently, but even with all the hurt and suffering those years apart caused, I hadn't been able to let her go. Not completely.

She groaned as I tilted her head to the side for better access.

My teeth closed on her bottom lip in a sharp nip that made her whimper. Fiona's hands came up, her fingers digging into the fabric of my shirt at my chest as her tongue met mine, stroke for stroke. It was the most intense, erotic kiss of my life. I never wanted it to end. Unfortunately a lack of oxygen forced us to eventually break apart.

I kept her in my arms, pressing my forehead against hers as I squeezed my eyes closed and struggled to fill my lungs with air.

"Baby, you have no fucking clue how long I've wanted to do that," I panted against her mouth. She jerked back just as I went in for another, breaking from my hold and taking several steps away. Her arms stretched out in front of her to keep me at a distance.

"Wh-what the hell was that?" she asked, breathing erratically. Her eyes flashed with something akin to panic, causing my blood to go cold in my veins.

"Fee—"

"I can't... I don't... I'm—Deacon, I'm not sure what's happening right now but that, that shouldn't have—"

"Don't," I growled, feeling like a knife had just been plunged into my stomach.

Her beautiful face fell, and her eyes flashed with gut-wrenching pity. I couldn't stand it. "Deacon," she whispered, her tone ragged. "You're my best friend."

And the hits just kept on coming. I shook my head to stop her. "No. Don't say that."

Fiona's hands came up in a placating gesture as she stepped in my direction. "It's true. Deacon, I feel like I only just got my friend back. I don't want to lose what we have again."

Moving backward, I lifted my arms to grasp the back of my neck as a humorless laugh escaped my throat. "Are you kidding me with this shit? You didn't seem to have a problem taking Grayson out of the friend zone," I spit out bitterly.

I stood motionless as her expression became awash with frustration and sorrow. "That's not fair," she said in a pained whisper.

"No, I get it. It's not you, it's me, right?" I snapped sarcastically. "It'll always be the other Lockhart brother, am I right?"

"Deacon, stop. It's not like—"

"I'm such a fucking idiot," I muttered it more to myself than to her. Spinning around, I started down the steps, vaguely noticing the sound of her footsteps trailing after me.

"Deacon, will you please wait. Just listen."

"I'm done with this bullshit, Fiona," I called over my shoulder. "Have a nice life."

With that, I climbed into my car, started it up, and laid on the gas, determined to put her and this goddamned night in my rearview permanently.

The calls and texts from her started the very next day, messages and voice mails begging me to talk. She even started showing up at my bar, sitting alone on a barstool, just waiting for me to give her a second of my time.

I never did.

It went on like that for months. Each call went unanswered, each text unreturned. Avoiding her at The Black Sheep was easy enough with all the people constantly around. But when I got home from closing down late one night and found her sitting in her car, waiting for me, that had been harder. Instead of acknowledging her presence, I pulled into the garage and went inside my house without so much as a backward glance.

That had done it. I got the text the next day informing me that she was giving up. I still had that goddamned message saved in my phone.

Fiona: *I get it. If I could go back to that night and do it all over again I would. I'm so sorry. I'll leave you alone.*

I would've been relieved if reading that hadn't hurt so

goddamn much. But what was done was done. And I was through letting her crush my heart over and over again.

"Hello. Earth to Deacon."

Leah's voice yanked me from the past and brought me back to the present.

"Sorry, what?"

I chanced a glance from the road in her direction to find her watching me closely. "You okay? You zoned out for a second."

"Yeah." I mentally shook off the filth of the memory and tried my best to concentrate on Leah, and only Leah. "Yeah, sorry. Everything's fine."

"Okay." The one word sounded skeptical, but fortunately she let it drop. "Look, I know you're probably tired of listening to me complain. I didn't ask to come today to start anything. I just... well, I like you, Deacon. And I know how important your friends are to you. I just worry that I don't stand a chance if they don't like me."

Grabbing her hand, I pulled it across the console and rested it on my thigh, using my thumb to rub gentle circles along her wrist. "I like you too," I spoke honestly. The shit with my friends aside, I had fun with Leah. She was sexy and smart. She made me laugh and was dynamite in bed. Three months wasn't enough time to really get to know a person, and I owed it to myself to see if there was someone out there I could picture spending my life with. "And I'll have a word with one of the guys. I'll get it taken care of."

Leah lifted my hand and placed a kiss on my knuckles. "Thanks, babe. Today will be great. You'll see. I'll win them over."

CHAPTER TWO

FIONA

WELL THIS JUST SUCKS.

What was I thankful for this Thanksgiving? That would be wine. Lots and lots of wine. It was the only thing that would get me through this shit-tastic holiday.

If I had known *exactly* who all was coming today, I'd have taken my parents up on their invitation to celebrate Thanksgiving with them at their cabin in the mountains. At least then I would've been able to see snow and not the crappy slushy rain we were currently dealing with in the city.

But no, once again I allowed my heart to override my head and decided to join my friends at Caleb and Daphne's house. Firstly, because I wanted as much snuggle time as I could get with their baby girl, Evie. There was just something about babies that turned me to mush. I couldn't get enough of that little girl. And my other friend Lola was currently pregnant with her and Grayson's first baby as well, so there was even more goodness to come.

It might have been awkward, spending the holiday with my ex, his pregnant wife and all their friends and family, but Lola was amazing. As soon as she realized I wasn't a threat to what she and Grayson were building, she'd pulled me into the fold. Her two best friends, Daphne and Sophia, had quickly become *my* friends as well. I was officially part of their crazy little tribe, and I felt like I'd been a part of it for years. I was comfortable there, I belonged.

But the main reason I decided to spend my first holiday without my folks was because *he* was going to be here. Deacon Lockhart. The man I'd stupid, stupid, stupidly not realized was the love of my life until it was too late.

I'd been told that it was strictly close friends and family coming to Thanksgiving. Then he showed up with his brand-new girlfriend in tow, effectively shattering my mood *and* my holiday spirit in one crushing blow.

It wasn't Deacon's fault though. I had absolutely no right being upset with him for moving on. I mean, he'd put himself out there after all, took a leap of faith and made his feelings for me known, but I'd been too much of a coward at the time to accept what he was offering me.

It wasn't that I didn't have feelings for him, because I did. And *that* was the problem. I'd dated his brother, for crying out loud. And it had been really serious at one time. I thought Grayson and I were on the road to marriage. What kind of woman bounced from one brother to the next?

I convinced myself that it was inappropriate to move on to Deacon—even though what I felt brewing in my blood for him was so much more intense than it had ever been with Grayson.

As everybody moved into the dining room to eat, I took the chance to suck back more wine before going to join them. Caleb was at the head of the table with Daphne to his right, their little girl in a highchair between the two of them. I sat next to Daphne while Sophia took the seat to my other side. I breathed a sigh of relief, thinking I was in the clear when Grayson sat to Caleb's left, placing Lola directly across from me. Unfortu-

About the Author

Thomas G. Fiffer, Executive Editor at The Good Men Project, is a graduate of Yale University and holds an M.A. in creative writing from the University of Illinois at Chicago. He is a professional writer, speaker, and storyteller with a focus on diagnosing and healing dysfunctional relationships. His book, **What Is Love: A Guide for the Perplexed to Matters of the Heart**, is available on Amazon. He is also working on his first novel.

Table of Contents

Introduction

Relationship hell is the worst, right? For anyone who's been there—and I know I'm not alone—there's nothing more heartbreaking than the sickening feeling of something warm growing cold, something sweet going sour, something compassionate turning contemptuous, something supportive becoming destructive, and your source of love and healing becoming the cause of toxic damage. Suddenly, what seemed to be working so well is not, like the shiny car you drive off the dealer's lot that collapses down the road in a heap of broken parts. "But I was just in heaven," you say. "How did I get to this infernal place?"

So begins the first paragraph of an article I wrote for **The Good Men Project** in March of 2014 that **instantly went viral** and has accumulated over 250,000 page views to date. Though I'm not a psychologist, marriage counselor, or social worker, I had an inkling—from my own painful life experience—that the piece would prove popular. But I had no idea my layman's description of dysfunctional relationships would resonate so widely and deeply and unleash a torrent of comments that left me simultaneously elated—because I had so successfully touched a raw, collective nerve—and wanting to cry—because these comments confirmed that so many people have clearly suffered and are still suffering in destructive relationships similar to my own that are ruining their lives. Here is a selection of comments that appeared both on Facebook and directly on the published article.

———

Stacey - "Wish I'd read this a long time ago when I was with someone that all 7 of these fit perfect!"

Linda - "Hit it on the head...."

Russell - "OMG! Wish I read this ten years ago!"

Gregory - "Wow, this is exactly on target! Been there, but no longer!"

Nicole - "Just got out of one and I must say everything you said was true of my situation!"

LHar - "Holy crap. Every single sentence applied."

Richard - "Wow! All these points are so recognizable!"

Moose - "Every single line was spot on with my life, I'm a success at work, nice home and car yet i'm a total mess on the inside."

Tom - "I have had to find the person I buried to be in this relationship and I'm still looking to find me. One step at a time...thank you for putting this into words."

Anonymous - "OMG...it's like reading my own words...about my own life! Here I am, sitting at my desk at work, waving my hands in the air while holding back tears. Thanks so much for letting me know I'm not alone!"

And then there was this shocker, from a woman who recognized the signs in herself.

Kristen Mae - "You have given me some things to think about as, sadly, I recognize myself in some of your points. That's embarrassing to admit, but I'm glad to have stumbled upon your piece. My husband will thank you (and I already do)."

But my three favorites are:

Sarah C. - "All 7 signs were present in my relationship with my ex-husband, and it took me catching him in my bed with another woman to realize what a piece of crap he was."

Stefanie - "The article was so much a mirror of my experience that it was simultaneously alarming ... and also therapeutic as I realized my suffering wasn't unique .... I wish I could reach my arms out to give the writer of this enlightening article and everyone who has endured a similar situation a big hug."

Sam - "This makes hindsight look like it's in HD."

———

I think Sam may have a career writing blurbs. Kidding aside, the overwhelming response motivated me to keep writing about relationships and how they go so dreadfully wrong—**first** because I had much more to say about each of the flash points I'd hit in The 7 Signs; **second** because I had learned, through my more than 10,000 hours during two dysfunctional marriages, effective strategies and tactics to deal with dysfunction; and **third**, because I wanted to spread the word about dysfunctional relationships to a wider audience to help people become aware that **the dynamics they're experiencing are not unique but actually fairly common**. This point cannot be emphasized enough.

Most people stuck in relationships that fit these distressing patterns believe they are the only ones (I know I did), that there's something wrong with them, that everyone else fares better with their partners, and worst of all that the hellish treatment they're experiencing is their own fault---because their partners have convinced, cajoled, bullied, and sometimes battered them into believing they're the cause.

And that's why they need this book.

I survived two marriages defined—and ultimately destroyed—by dysfunctional dynamics, and it took me a long time to learn and break the patterns that were preventing me from being happy. So if you know someone who needs to read this book, please let them know about it. It may be exactly what they need to read. One of the articles included here, "7 Things I Wish I'd Known Before My Two Crazy Marriages," caused one reader to comment, "Thomas, your piece took my breath away. I guess it shouldn't come as a surprise to me how common our human experiences are, and yet, what you wrote could have been my words verbatim."

It is important to note that many of the dysfunctional behaviors and patterns discussed in this book accompany mental illnesses such as bi-polar disorder and personality disorders including narcissistic personality disorder (NPD) and borderline personality disorder (BPD) that have been thoroughly explored by other authors. I'm not a doctor or practitioner—just a keen observer of human nature—and this book is not an exploration of or diagnostic key for mental illness, the diagnosis and treatment of which are best left to medical professionals. But it does provide a solid, experiential, and helpful framework for getting a handle on the patterns that tear couples apart. When a relationship is dysfunctional as in, **not working, not serving your best interests, and causing you constant pain**, you don't have time for a battery of tests or to seek the perfect label. Your life is ticking away minute by miserable minute, hour by hellish hour, day by destructive day, and you need to move quickly to **recognize the problem, identify the source, and take decisive action** —either to right the ship or abandon it. This book helps readers do just that—by gently but assertively revealing the painful truths about dysfunctional relationships, reminding them that romantic partnerships are supposed to be a healthy source of love and support, and letting them know it's OK to walk away.

I would like to offer special thanks to The Good Men Project and my cherished colleagues there for providing me with a supportive forum for my writing and encouraging me to tell my story. Thanks also to Ina Chadwick, for giving me my storytelling breakthrough and to Theresa Byrne, for helping me see the relevance of my personal experience to readers and giving me the push to start sharing.

The 7 Deadly Signs of a Dysfunctional Relationship

How to recognize the signs of a rotten relationship—before it's too late.

———

Relationship hell is the worst, right? For anyone who's been there—and I know I'm not alone—there's nothing more heartbreaking than the sickening feeling of something warm growing cold, something sweet going sour, something compassionate turning contemptuous, something supportive becoming destructive, and your source of love and healing becoming the cause of toxic damage. Suddenly, what seemed to be working so well is not, like the shiny car you drive off the dealer's lot that collapses down the road in a heap of broken parts. "But I was just in heaven," you say. "How did I get to this infernal place?"

Some relationships are troubled from the start—and we know it. But the deeply dysfunctional ones, the ones we get subtly and unwittingly enmeshed in that have the potential to shatter our lives, tend to start off smoothly and are often dreamy at the beginning. You know, that feeling of, "Oh my God, I'm so lucky. I've actually found the perfect partner who loves everything about me—and thinks I have no faults at all!" When this happens, watch out. You're so head-over-heels in love that you may fail to see the warning signs—some small like a pebble in your shoe that you dismiss as minor, some glaring like giant red flags flapping in the wind that you blissfully ignore—that you're strapping yourself into a demonic roller coaster for a life-threatening ride.

The up stretch of the roller coaster feels great, and then … whoa! … the bottom drops out and you're in free fall. There's screaming all right, but it's not from excitement. It's the angry shrieks of you and your partner fighting with the same passionate intensity you brought to your romance. After a while, the ups and downs become so tortuous and harrowing that all you want is a slow, straight, comfortable journey. All you crave … is peace.

◆◇◆

Here are my seven deadly signs of dysfunction—drawn from experience—that set in fairly quickly after the honeymoon is over. Dysfunctional relationships have the distressing tendency to grow more and more difficult to escape as they progress, and we adopt and ultimately become invested in maintaining increasingly unhealthy coping mechanisms to survive. Recognizing these seven signs when they start happening can save you from worlds of hurt and help you make an early exit from a relationship you will later regret.

◆◇◆

1. Tedium: You have the same argument over and over again and never resolve it. This is perhaps the most obvious sign that something is wrong. Communication stops working. Agreement on almost anything becomes impossible. You each have different versions of reality, and they collide with the force of a supersonic jet smashing into a nuclear-powered forcefield. Things you did two weeks or two months or even two years ago get endlessly rehashed—from failing to take the garbage out if you live together to not remembering the first anniversary of your second date. And there's no end to it. The two of you go at it like boxers in the ring, but there's no final bell and no decision, not even a TKO. You just keep socking away at each other until one of you falls to the mat with no more strength to stand.

2. Blame: Everything is always your fault. And I mean everything. Dysfunctional partners avoid accountability like the plague. They twist and turn situations around, revise the narrative, edit out what doesn't serve them, and even gaslight you to make their unhappiness not only your fault but also your responsibility to fix. Unhappy childhood? You have to replace the love they didn't get. Weak father or mother? You have to become the dragon slayer who rights all the wrongs—real or imagined—that have ever been done to them. Anger management issues? You just need to stop making your partner so upset—which means you have to stop drawing boundaries, speaking truth, expressing your feelings, and being yourself.

3. Guilt: You're constantly apologizing, even for things you didn't do. Keeping the peace requires you to suck it up—every single time. It becomes a joke, the way you take the fall for everything, but it's not funny, and you begin to feel worthless and ashamed. Your partner's angry reactions become justified, and the increasingly unreasonable demands become givens, with any resistance viewed as disloyalty and cause for character assassination. Forgot to make the morning coffee, or you were just too tired? You're screwed. Made a date with a friend but didn't put it on the calendar? You're an insensitive bastard or bitch. Talked on the phone to the family member your partner hates? You're in for a rough night. The words "I'm sorry" escape your lips so many times that you start your sentences with them, even when you know in your heart you haven't done anything wrong.

4. Tension: When things are good, you're waiting for the other shoe to drop. My therapist used to encourage me to use the calm times to address the stuff that happened when things were crazy. I was always reluctant, because I wanted to enjoy the calm times and avoid starting a fight. The thing is, you can never truly enjoy the good periods when you're in a dysfunctional relationship, because these often infrequent bright spots are inevitably darkened by fear of the bleakness and blackness you know is coming—no matter what you do to prevent it. You try to relax when you're not fighting, on a day when everything seems to go right, or during a conflict-free stretch of time accomplished by your sacrificing every principle, squashing your ego into a tight little ball, and stifling every instinct to scream, but you're living in constant, anxious terror of the next confrontation, and what's worse, you have no idea what's going to light the fuse of that bomb.

5. Uncertainty: You never know who's going to be there when you get home. One night, your partner is sweet, kind, and forgiving. The next, you can do no right. From the moment you walk in the door, the ogre is determined to make you feel like crap about yourself, chop you up in little pieces, serve you up for stew, then spit you out with disgust. You live on the edge, and you're constantly monitoring your every move, your every word, your tone of voice, as well as taking preventive measures—sometimes involving extreme humbling, unwise spending, or both—to ensure a welcoming reception. You leave work undone and come home early. You spend half your paycheck on a piece of jewelry. Or you cook a favorite dinner, hoping all the plates and glasses won't get smashed. Whatever you do, it's a crapshoot, with even odds you'll have the best sex of your life or wish you were living in a quiet monastery or convent as far away as possible from your partner.

6. Frustration: Getting even the simplest things done is hugely complicated. Despite your best efforts, you're always butting heads and can't work with your partner as a team. If you try to lead, you're attacked. If you try to follow, you're never doing enough of the scutwork. Making decisions together is so hard because rationality gets thrown out the window. Your partner's agenda flows from ego, insecurity, past hurts, and unhealthy needs, while you're a) trying to be practical, b) getting mocked for your suggestions, c) being told you suck at decision-making, and d) all of the above. What's even worse is that you eventually give up on trying to make things happen with your partner and a) assume the burden yourself, b) invent unhealthy workarounds to get things done, c) fill with resentment over everything falling on your shoulders, or d) all of the above.

7. Hopelessness: You feel like there's a dark cloud over your life that won't go away—a permanent weather system that obscures the sun. This is the saddest feeling of all. You lose your optimism, your light, the spark that keeps you going. You feel oppressed, and even though you want to get out, you convince yourself that you can't, that this is your fate, your lot in life, that you're just meant to suffer. You start to drink the Kool-Aid that your partner is serving, the stuff about how you really were a pretty lousy person before you got together, and you're being trained now in how to make someone happy. Never mind that you had happy, fulfilling friendships and relationships before this one. Your partner has already told you what was wrong with those friends and former lovers and probably tried to cut them all out of your life. Your mission —and there's no choice but to accept it—is to sacrifice yourself to make a miserable person occasionally happy, to stand with your finger in the dyke until it rots from gangrene and falls off, to bear the unbearable, to sustain the unsustainable, and best of all—to like it, to enjoy it, to be grateful for the opportunity to be with such a demanding person who gives you so little in return.

Does any of this strike a chord? Do any of these examples resonate? If the answer is yes, you've gotten yourself into a seriously dangerous situation that threatens your emotional security and leaves you vulnerable to leading a life of co-dependent enslavement. If any or all of these things are happening in your relationship, go get some help. Read some books about co-dependency, emotional abuse, and the types of mental health conditions—particularly narcissistic and borderline personality disorder—that enable dysfunctional relationships to thrive. Equally important, start believing in yourself, in what your heart tells you is right, healthy, and true. And don't worry about betraying your partner or letting your partner down by telling someone—a friend, family member, or professional—what you're experiencing. Most of all, take the following words to heart. Write them down or type them up and put them somewhere you will see them every day.

"Getting out is not giving up on someone when staying is giving up on yourself."

When Your Partner Stops Giving: The Silent Pain of Emotional Withholding

The suffering caused by emotional withholding can be more excruciating than verbal or even physical abuse. How to recognize it—and what to do.

———

Confession: I've been holding out on you. When I wrote The 7 Deadly Signs of a Dysfunctional Relationship, I left out the eighth: emotional withholding. A reader pointed this out in a haunting comment. Sara wrote:

> *What's missing from this discussion is the kind of dysfunction that isn't tyrannical but instead quietly sucks out your integrity and self-respect because there are NO fights or fireworks. This is the passive-death non-relationship in which every dissatisfaction you express is completely ignored or casually dismissed. Not with a bang but a whimper……….*

Wow. Right? In my response to Sara's comment I directed her to a post I'd published on my blog a while back on emotional withholding. It starts out like this:

> *If you've lived with a dysfunctional partner, chances are you've experienced it.*

Coldness replaces warmth.
Silence replaces conversation.
Turning away replaces turning towards.
Dismissiveness replaces receptivity.
And contempt replaces respect.

Emotional withholding is, I believe, the toughest tactic to deal with when trying to create and maintain a healthy relationship, because it plays on our deepest fears—rejection, unworthiness, shame and guilt, the worry that we've done something wrong or failed or worse, that there's something wrong with us.

But Sara's description is more accurate and compelling than mine. Her line, "quietly sucks out your integrity and self-respect" is still stuck in my head three days later. It makes me think of those films where an alien creature hooks up a human to some ghastly, contorted machine and drains him of his life force drop by drop, or those horrible "can't watch" scenes where witches swoop down and inhale the breath of children to activate their evil spells of world domination. In the movies, the person in peril always gets saved. The thieves are vanquished. The deadly transfusion halted. And the heroic victim recovers. But in real life, in real dysfunctional relationships, there's often no savior and definitely no guarantee of a happy ending. Your integrity and self-respect can indeed be hoovered out, turning you into an emotional zombie, leaving you like one of the husks in the video game Mass Effect, unable to feel pain or joy, a mindless, quivering animal, a soulless puppet readily bent to the Reapers' will.

Emotional withholding is so painful because it is the absence of love, the absence of caring, compassion, communication, and connection.

You're locked in the meat freezer with the upside-down carcasses of cows and pigs, shivering, as your partner casually walks away from the giant steel door.

You're desperately lonely, even though the person who could comfort you by sharing even one kind word is right there, across from you at the dinner table, seated next to you at the movie, or in the same bed with you, back turned, deaf to your words, blind to your agony, and if you dare to reach out, scornful of your touch.

When you speak, you might as well be talking to the wall, because you're not going to get an answer, except maybe, if you're lucky, a dismissive shrug. And the more you talk about anything that matters to you, the more you try to assert that you matter, the more likely your withholding partner is to belittle or ignore what you're saying and leave you in the cold.

Awful but true—you actually wish for the fight, the fireworks that Sara points out are not flashing, because even a shouting match, an ugly scene, would involve an exchange of words, because even physical conflict would constitute physical connection, because fire, even if it burns you, is preferable to ice.

Imagine saying something three, four, even five times to your partner and receiving no response. Or maybe, you get a grunt. You ask yourself, am I here? Do I mean anything to this person? Do I matter? Do I even exist? If you cry alone on the polar icecap of emotional withholding, and there's no one there to hear you, did you actually make a sound?

Your accomplishments go unrecognized, your contributions unmentioned, your presence at best grudgingly acknowledged, and any effort at bridging the chasm is spurned. The rope you throw over the crevasse lashes back at you, whipping in the winter wind.

You become pathetic—pleading, begging, literally on your knees, apologizing for everything, offering things that are distasteful to you, promising to be better, just to re-secure your partner's affection.

But you're like the dying Eskimo elder, wrapped in sealskin and placed on an ice floe to float away into the great beyond. Only you're screaming, "I'm not dying! I'm not even sick! I'm perfectly healthy!" as your partner's silence speaks the words, "You're dead to me." And death, death enters your consciousness as an option. Death begins to feel like a viable alternative, a way to achieve relief from the unbearable pain.

Emotional withholding is typically a response to your trying to stand up for yourself, to an assertion of your rights within the relationship. And perhaps the deepest pain of all comes from your partner's insistence that you deserve to be treated this way, deserve to be punished, and, to paraphrase my older post, your partner's absurd argument that if you just give up your silly notion of having a healthy, communicative relationship between two equal partners and resubmit to emotional domination and abuse, the caring, compassion, communication, and connection, the warmth and the love, will return.

◆◇◆

And they might—for five minutes, five hours, even five days—until you assert your yourself again.

◆◇◆

The truth is, caring, compassion, communication, connection, warmth, and love should NEVER be conditional and NEVER be willfully withheld, EVER, unless the relationship is already over and you need to draw a boundary to establish your new life and preserve your own sanity. Withholding these within a relationship is abuse, a kind of emotional blackmail, no different from the other kind that threatens to hurt you where you're most vulnerable if you don't comply with your partner's desires or needs. But the harder you work towards creating a healthy relationship, the more your dysfunctional partner will withhold the very things on which the health of the relationship depends. This is how your relationship becomes "the passive-death non-relationship" that Sara mentions, and you feel emptied instead of filled, hollowed instead of hallowed, sunk under the weight of scorn and silence instead of buoyed by the lift of love.

◆◇◆

Confession: When your partner withholds, after a while you give up and start doing it too. This creates the death-spiral in which both partners abandon the relationship, slink into siege mode behind the walls of their fortresses, and try to starve each other out until someone capitulates, crawling forward with parched throat on withered limbs, begging for a sip of water and a scrap of food.

There's only one way to deal effectively with a partner who withholds from you, and it's this: **You must make it clear that the relationship is OVER, FOREVER, if your partner does not start acknowledging you and communicating.** This is the only tactic that has a chance of working, because the withholding partner doesn't actually want the relationship to end. Your tormentor is deriving too much satisfaction out of dispensing punishment and seeing you suffer. Why you might want to remain with a sadist is your own business, but if you do want to try to save it, you have to threaten to leave and be willing to make good on your word if things don't improve quickly. And if they do improve, you have to insist that you will be out the door if it ever, ever happens again.

21 Signs Your Relationship Is Doomed

We all know relationships are hard work, but they're not supposed to be hell. These 21 tell-tale signs spell perdition for even the most committed couples.

———

Love does not begin and end
the way we seem to think it does.
Love is a battle, love is a war; love is a growing up.

- James Baldwin

The thrill is gone
The thrill is gone away
The thrill is gone baby
The thrill is gone away

- B.B. King

———

Unless we truly know it's over, we never want to believe it. The "I'm done" moment is usually recognized in hindsight. Sure, we've been hurt, even grievously wounded, but there's always hope, there's always faith. When turned towards the positive, hope and faith are powerful forces and miraculous sources of healing, but when employed as mechanisms of denial, they form the pillars of a delusional world, along with their companion—fantasy. Quitting is a dirty word, and it's drilled into us that we should never give up. Knowing when it's right to quit, when it's best to move on, is the key to your emotional survival, and these 21 signs can help you come to terms with the heartbreaking realization that what once was is no more and is never going to be. As a rule, if you can say yes to four or more of these in your relationship, it's time to close the book and begin a new chapter.

1. Resentment. Are you suffering silently, taking your lumps, gritting your teeth, and never directly confronting your partner over behaviors that make you angry? You may think you're saving the relationship by not speaking up, but you're actually flooding yourself with resentment that will inevitably overflow. Don't fool yourself into believing your reservoir is unlimited. The tipping point will come, and your resentment will influence your own behavior, in ways you may not even be aware of, leading you to get back at your partner and drive the death stake into the relationship. When resentment moves in, communication has moved out, and there's little hope for reconciliation.

2. Disrespect. If you or your partner have reached the point of showing disrespect or being dismissive of each other, forget it. There's no quicker way to erode good will and make it easy for someone to stop loving you. People may keep their bodies in the room if they're treated badly

—particularly in the cycle of abuse—but their hearts and minds soon check out, and the relationship becomes a hollow shell.

3. Contempt. Marriage expert John Gottman cites contempt as the deadliest of his "four horsemen" (the others are criticism, defensiveness, and stonewalling) and claims he can tell if a marriage will fail by watching a couple for just 15 minutes. I know whereof he speaks. Contempt is like liquid nitrogen. A cold look of scorn from the one who's supposed to warm your heart means you've fallen through the ice and you're drowning in the frozen pond, and no, your partner is not going to save you.

4. Lying. There's lying to your partner and lying to yourself. Neither protects your partner or the relationship. Pretending you still love someone and speaking false words to mask your betrayal doesn't insulate your partner from harm; it only delays and magnifies the damage. Similarly, pretending you're happy and convincing yourself, against your heart and better judgment that everything is OK constitutes an abandonment of self and a withdrawal from reality. If you can't stay grounded in the here and now, the relationship can't thrive.

5. Mistrust. Do you really think it's wise to be with someone you can't trust? Do we have to say more about this one?

6. Badmouthing. Anything good you have to say about your partner should be said in public. Anything bad is best kept private, unless you're on your way out and confiding in your family or close friends. Public badmouthing, even if it's meant as a joke or petty complaining, is the tip of an iceberg of deep dissatisfaction that can sink your relationship to the bottom of the sea.

7. Distancing. When you find yourself tuning out, seeking distractions, and making a conscious effort to avoid connection and intimacy, it's time to step away from the source of your pain. You might still wear each other's rings or live under the same roof, but if you've severed the emotional bond or you're slowly letting it unravel, you may as well make a clean break.

8. Demanding proofs of love. "If you loved me, you would . . ." Allowing this absurd request to rule your life is so tempting. After all, it's often so easy just to get it over with and do the thing your partner asks. But what your partner is really saying is, "I don't believe, trust, or accept your love unless you go through this hoop for me." It's not actually a proof of your love, but a way of soothing your partner's anxiety and addressing the feeling that he or she is unlovable, and soon enough the hoop becomes a ring of fire. The only person who can change those feelings of unlovability is their owner, and asking you to do it is a sign your partner is mentally unwell.

9. Public humiliation. Has your partner ever shamed you in public, with outrageous behavior, by airing dirty laundry, or by accusing or severely mistreating you? An apology will always follow, but it wasn't an accident or the result of too much drinking, and despite the promises, it will be repeated. It's evidence of a fragile ego and deep-seated self-hatred. No amount of love you give can make someone love themselves, and without help, your partner will only make you more and more miserable.

10. Obsession with another person. If one partner is obsessed with someone outside the relationship—either a potential love interest or even a best friend—there's a good chance that availability and connection have broken down within the relationship. It's healthy not to have all the energy directed inward, but your partner must remain your primary focus. Obsession also indicates an unmet need, but it's likely one you can't meet for your partner.

11. Obsession with pornography. The jury is out, but some find a little bit of smut, enjoyed together, to be a turn-on. Watching others can also be a way for couples to express their fantasies and get in touch with what they want in bed. But obsessive consumption of porn by one or both partners is a sign that satisfaction will always elude that person, and the quest for the holy grail—or multl-orgasmic image—will lead down a road of extreme perversion.

12. Emotional infidelity. A one-night stand with a colleague on a business trip, a brief fling with the hot personal trainer, distasteful and devastating as these are, they need not be relationship killers. Sexual monogamy is hard and not necessarily hard-wired. The first question a partner inevitably asks when the indiscretion is discovered or disclosed is "Do you love him/her?" It's transference of the emotional attachment we fear the most, because emotional intimacy is the core of a relationship and makes everything else possible.

13. Inability to resolve conflict. This manifests first as endless fighting without reaching agreement and after a while morphs into the "whatever" stage, in which partners stop caring about the outcome because they've stopped investing in the relationship. There's something to be said for the maxim of never going to bed angry. If neither partner can be the bigger person, give up the need to be right, and approach conflict in a conciliatory fashion, there's no point in continuing.

14. Sabotage. When we do things unconsciously that damage our relationship, it's our psyche telling us we want and need out. You can say you want to stay until you're blue in the face, but your actions will always speak louder than your words.

15. Addictive behaviors. If your partner is a substance abuser, a compulsive spender or gambler, a sex addict, or even a true workaholic, your relationship will never take first priority. And unless it does, you won't be happy. Not to mention that addictive behaviors, especially when enabled, can ruin lives.

16. Unhealthy attachments. Is your partner still attached to an ex-spouse or former lover or enmeshed with his or her family? These attachments can disrupt and ultimately destroy the fabric of a healthy relationship, eating holes in it until it disintegrates. Honor thy mother and father. Respect thine exes, especially if you've had children with them. But always put your partner first. If you feel like you're second fiddle—or fifth violin—it's time to face the music.

17. Threats and emotional blackmail. These should never, ever occur in a healthy relationship. They are often presented as being about love but they are always about control. Period. And control is a form of abuse. Period. Run from these as fast as you can.

18. Comparisons and ratings. Is your partner comparing you to others—people who earn more, look more attractive, or have a better personality? Or rating your attributes on a scale? This is a form of denigration. If someone thinks the grass is greener, or that they won't have to fertilize and pull weeds in another field, let them go for it, and let them go. We're each unique individuals, and how we measure up against another or some arbitrary standard isn't relevant. In a nod to number 8: if your partner loved you, he or she wouldn't do that.

19. Indifference. Honestly. Why stay if you no longer care?

20. Withdrawal of affection. There's nothing wrong with wanting a roommate, but if you want more from your relationship, don't stay with a partner who has become one.

21. Physical violence. Never acceptable under any circumstances. No excuses. No explanations. No justifications. No more.

◆◇◆

Ultimately, in my opinion, all relationship conflict and the behavior that accompanies it springs from pain. If the conflict is an attempt to open and cleanse a wound, to promote healing, to mend holes, strengthen the bond and bring partners closer together,—then you have a "fighting" chance. But if it is an effort to rend and tear apart, to bash and smash and break, to assuage one's own pain by causing pain for another, the writing is on the wall. We'd best read it, or we'll end up weeping.

5 Signs You're Being Played by a 'Victim'

How to know when a 'victim-player' is playing you and how to recognize a true survivor.

———

Well you are such an easy evil
Such a sensuous sin
Sometimes I don't know where I'm going
'Till I've been taken in

- Alan O'Day, *Easy Evil*

———

We've all heard their sad stories and been sucked into the tragedy and drama. They have an unfair boss. Or horrible parents. Or a back-stabbing best friend. Or an ex bent on their destruction. And sometimes—all of the above. They spin a sob story to profess their innocence, confirm their helplessness, and engage our sympathy. They never tell us what they did—their role in the saga—or what they are doing about it, other than nursing their wounds and plotting revenge, but focus instead on what's been done to them and what they wish someone (that someone soon to be revealed as us) would do about it.

Let's call these people victim players, or VPs for short. And let's make an important distinction between real victims, people who have suffered hurt and abuse at the hands of others—particularly those they trusted—and VPs who, while they may have experienced real injury, devote the bulk of their energy to playing the role of the victim and reaping the rewards it affords instead of pursuing healing to become functional and whole.

Below are five red flags that will help you determine when a VP is playing you, along with five contrasting traits of true survivors.

1. Grandiose rewards for small acts. The VP's strategy starts small, and that's what hooks you. You're asked to do a minor favor, something seemingly innocuous and inconsequential that causes you little trouble or expense. Perhaps it's picking something up on your way home from work, doing some Internet research, or making a quick call. Often, there is something inappropriate about the request—such as calling in sick to the unfair boss on the VP's behalf—but whatever it is, it won't require much effort. Then comes the reward. A huge bunch of flowers. Theater tickets. An expensive bottle of wine. A gift utterly out of scale with your action that lets you know just how much it meant to the VP. Small investment, huge reward. Sweet deal, right? Well, bait isn't called bait because it's sour and unattractive. The next request will be a bit bigger, and the reward somewhat smaller, given humbly as all the VP can afford right now. Then come the IOUs, which the VP's strapped circumstances will make you hesitate to cash in on. Your reward is now the relief of the VPs anxiety and the feel-good you get from helping someone "in need." And the cycle is just beginning.

2. Hero worship. As you become the VP's helper, your stature grows to heroic proportions. You are the knight in shining armor, the dragon-slayer, the indispensable one, and the one who can do no wrong—at least, until you refuse a request. Don't be fooled by the VP's false worry about how much stress he or she is causing you, how much he or she owes you, the sacrifices you're starting to make in your own life, or statements that turbo-boost your ego and make you feel superhuman. The VP is playing out a well-rehearsed dysfunctional pattern, and while you're being put on a pedestal now, you're being set up for a big fall.

3. Progressive transfer of responsibilities. Pretty soon, you're doing things for the VP that he or she is perfectly capable of handling—and frankly should be—and you may start to feel used. There's always a reason, an excuse, a mitigating factor that prevents the VP from, say, picking up kids from school or camp, shopping for groceries (you shop, you pay), dealing with family issues or finances, even co-parenting with an ex. Eventually, all these tasks and more begin to fall on your capable shoulders. It's one thing to be helpful to someone. It's another entirely to enable them. The VP has chosen you carefully because you fail to make this distinction. Your involvement deepens to the point that removing yourself

—which at times you consider—would devastate the VP, leaving him or her to fend for herself in a cruel world filled with uncaring friends and vicious enemies. The hook was barbed, and now you're stuck, because pulling it out will cause you pain—the pain of abandoning a person who depends on you—along with hurting the VP, who, you conveniently forget, got along just fine before you came along.

4. Use of guilt, bullying, and emotional blackmail to gain compliance. By now, your own life is in turmoil. You're having to make uncomfortable tradeoffs, to choose between serving your master and attending to your needs, which seem to pale in comparison to the VPs. Your parents want you to come for dinner, but the VP is having a crisis. Your child needs help with homework, but the VP has to unload the horrors of the day. Your friends want to get together over the weekend, but you've got an

errand list a mile long. And forget about taking a walk or
going to the gym. You actually feel selfish when you think
of yourself, and the VP magnifies this by minimizing your
needs and accusing you of selfishness. "How can you
think of seeing your parents at a time like this?"
"Homework is not a crisis." "Are your friends more
important than painting my porch?" "All you ever do is go
to the gym. What about me?" You may hear shades of
narcissism in these statements, and many VPs display
narcissistic tendencies. If you insist on your own agenda
and refuse to do the VPs bidding, you will be badgered
unendingly and threatened—either by the prospect of the
VP's life collapsing without you and this demise being
your fault, or with horribly unpleasant consequences.
Chances are the VP has gotten you to reveal a few
secrets and vulnerabilities, and these can and will be
used against you to keep you in the game. Compromising
your position at work, lying about you to friends and
family, or flaming you on social media are typical threats
the VP uses with great success, and it is your own fear of
acknowledging being stuck and calling out the VP for
what he or she is that keeps you a prisoner.

5. Character assassination. This is the death blow that
ensures your enslavement. At first, you were a hero. Now,
you are no better than all the rest, in fact, worse than all
the rest, a selfish, uncaring, ungrateful asshole, a pathetic
excuse for a human being, a dick, a pussy, a bitch, a c**t.
If you were up on cloud nine before, you've now
descended to the deepest pit of hell. You thought you
were a good person, but a good person doesn't hurt a

poor victim who's been badly hurt before, trampled to near death, and who trusted that good person and asked for assistance. Now the VP has you by the short hairs, because your need to be good outweighs your need to be sensible. Seeing yourself as bad, as a wounder or abandoner, no different from the ones you and the VP commiserated about, proves too much for your psyche. You implode, and the carefully built walls of your life, which the VP so skillfully encouraged you to erode, collapse in on you and bury you under the rubble. Without help, there is no escape.

In contrast to the five red flags that reveal a VP, the five traits below are common to true survivors, people who have been through tragedy and determined not to let it define them.

1. Resilience. Survivors are fighters. They overcome things, and they are proud of their accomplishments. They don't get upset over small stuff and don't manufacture crises. They're already part of a supportive community, and they get appropriate help if and when they need it. A survivor doesn't need to enslave a pawn, as he or she himself may have been similarly trapped. The very thought is distasteful.

2. Genuine concern for your welfare. If a survivor asks you for a favor—small or large—your own needs will be considered, and there will be an option to refuse with no guilt. A survivor does not try to overstep your boundaries and fully expects you to maintain them.

3. Progressive self-reliance. A survivor has determined to leave being a victim behind. A survivor may need a lot of help walking in the beginning, but each step is a step towards greater independence. The last thing he or she wants is to dwell on the past (though it remains haunting) and to depend on another person for emotional or financial security.

4. Appropriate appreciation. A survivor says thank you in a way that's commensurate with your contribution. You will feel gratified, not overwhelmed.

5. Engaging you in their healing process. This is the ultimate sign of friendship. A survivor considers you truly helpful and a blessing not if you enable dysfunction and dependence but if you participate as a partner on the journey of healing.

This Guy Makes Your Abuser Look Good

Abuse doesn't always fit the stereotypes, which makes it difficult to recognize and act on.

———

A while back I wrote a blog post called "Call It What It Is." I write a lot about dysfunctional relationships, and I wanted to educate people about domestic abuse, a subject with which I am intimately familiar, both in my own life and the lives of my friends. Being a writer—and a writerly writer—I thought if I could redefine the vocabulary of abuse, I could redefine people's understanding of what constitutes abusive behavior and shatter a prevailing preconception: that abuse is always characterized by extreme anger and physical violence, a preconception that leads to untold suffering by causing people to pretend that what's happening in their own lives and the lives of others doesn't qualify as abuse, because it doesn't look like the guy in the picture.

Abuse is a tricky topic to talk about and I got tripped up in words. I hid behind them, the same way so many victims hide behind a wall of denial and shame when bad stuff, really bad stuff, is happening to them.

So I'm going to try again. And instead of writing clever catch phrases like "abusive is not the new cranky, violent is not the new passionate, and borderline is not the new mercurial," I'm going to connect with my outrage over what I've seen and continue to see.

I'm going to speak from experience and tell you that the man who puts on a suit every morning over the white undershirt washed, folded, and laid out for him by his wife, who goes to his well-paid job where he checks their bank account hourly for any signs of his wife's purchases, who flies into a rage over her latte at Starbucks, who ignores her texts and phone calls all day, then comes home expecting a hot meal but withholds attention and affection from her, choosing instead to play endless video games, but never slaps her – I can tell you that this man is an abuser.

And I can tell you that the woman married to a man who earns a good six-figure income, who does more than his share of childcare, who serves with distinction on community boards, and who is in splendid physical shape for his age, the same woman who shops compulsively, calls her husband a failure, chastises him for not earning enough, demeans him in front of his children, and hits him below the belt without laying a finger on his person – I can tell you that this woman, too, is an abuser.

I can tell you that abusers can be handsome and pretty and rich and successful and invisibly malevolent and at times ever so confusingly loving and kind.

I can tell you that abusers can strike devastating blows by raising not their fists but a solitary eyebrow.

And I can tell you that abusers can torture their victims more viciously with silence than the cruelest of words.

I can tell you that abusers can be sitting at the next restaurant table, inhabiting the next cubicle, even living right next door.

The man who forces his wife to order fish instead of steak because she's on a diet. He's an abuser.

The colleague who gets off the phone with her husband and badmouths him to the whole office. She's an abuser.

The neighbor who always smiles politely, buys his wife a fancy car and showers her with jewels and perfume to brighten her look of dull resignation and mask the smell of persistent fear. He's an abuser.

The husband who says, "You know you love it, you know you want it," and does it even though his wife doesn't want it but doesn't refuse it. He's an abuser.

The girlfriend who pries her boyfriend away from his family and friends and gradually erodes those relationships, because she "loves him so much" and wants him all to herself. She's an abuser.

The partner whose constant and cruel dismissiveness causes his spouse to doubt her opinions, her intelligence, and ultimately her own sanity. He's an abuser.

And I can tell you that these abusers successfully convince the whole world—even their victim's friends and families—that the abused person is the one doing the hurting, that the abuser is only reacting to being hurt, and that the abused person deserved, yes deserved, what he or she got.

I can go one step further and tell you, yes you, to take a good, hard look in the mirror. To run your own behaviors against a checklist or two. To see if you match any of the profiles, if you engage in any or many of the telltale patterns that constitute abuse—but only if you're willing to be brutally honest. And if you're here, on this website, reading this article, there's a good chance you might.

There, I've unsheathed the knife, and gone for the jugular —the way an abuser would. I've raised my fist in outrage, and tried to throw the knockout punch—the way an abuser would. I've cocked the gun, and …

Enough with the words already. Here's my parting shot— fired at both abuse victims who are often unaware of what they're dealing with, and at the apologists who enable abuse (particularly non-physical) by downplaying the damage and dismissing the victims' cries for help with statements such as, "Well, it isn't really that bad," or "At least he didn't hit you." You know, the ones who listen impatiently to stories of a friend's suffering, shake their heads, gladly pay for the coffee or drinks, then drive away and do nothing.

Minimizing, marginalizing, and helping others make excuses for abusive behavior of any kind is no different from condoning that behavior and allowing it to continue.

And just because your partner isn't slamming you against a wall or verbally eviscerating you every night, that doesn't mean you aren't a victim—and ultimately a survivor—of serious, even criminally punishable domestic abuse. A nasty scowl, a dismissive remark, a jocular insult, really any sign of disrespect, much less contempt, all these are the tip of an unfathomable iceberg that freezes, then violently shatters any hope of intimacy, emotional security, and happiness in a relationship.

Abuse is endemic, if not epidemic. I don't need to cite numbers, like 1 in 3 women or 1 in 4 men. I'm an English major, as you may have figured, but even I can do the math. When it comes to abuse, one plus one is not two. One isolated, unrepeated incident of reactive anger can be explained, forgiven, and effectively prevented going forward. But one plus one, that makes a pattern. And my son taught me something he learned in second grade—the grade I skipped because I was considered to be so "gifted." A lesson I failed to learn early on. A pattern … is something that repeats itself.

5 Lies That Keep Us Stuck in Dysfunctional Relationships

At the core of dysfunctional relationships are five lies we tell ourselves.

———

A while back I wrote an article called The 7 Deadly Signs of a Dysfunctional Relationship. It immediately went viral and has now been viewed over 250,000 times, but don't click to read it now—just bookmark it for later. Because what I'm about to share with you is much more important and will change everything you know about dysfunctional relationships—and I mean everything—in an instant.

Here's the truth you already know: relationships can be the absolute best or absolute worst things that ever happen to you. You've probably been through at least one of each, and one that's gone from one extreme to the other. They're like the little girl in the Longfellow poem: when they're good, they're good indeed, and when they're bad, they're horrid. Our first reaction when things get horrld Is perfectly predictable: we blame our partner for the problems. 100%. Because we're "innocent." And because we're "victims." Functional couples learn to move past blame and self-victimization, to work on their issues in a cooperative context, and to change the ineffective, destructive way they communicate—a shift that has as much or more impact on happiness than the way partners act towards each other. Dysfunctional couples do the opposite. They invest heavily in the narrative of blame, sinking countless hours of fighting into it and endless floods of tears, as blaming the other becomes the narrative of the relationship. Any challenge to that fiction, any truth that would absolve the blamed partner to some degree and make the blaming partner even minimally accountable challenges the entire premise on which the relationship is based and therefore cannot be tolerated or accepted. In some cases, both partners continue bickering and blaming all the way to the grave.

We know that two people making opposite arguments can't both be right, but they can both be wrong. And they —meaning you—are both wrong. Because all accountability and responsibility for addressing and changing the dysfunction in your relationships rests entirely with you. That's right. It's all on your head. I'm not saying your partner doesn't drive you crazy, set off your triggers, and contribute to your own personal hell on earth. And I'm not saying you're ever responsible for another person abusing you. I am saying that blaming your partner and investing your energy in trying to get that person to change will never, ever, make things better. For any hope of happiness, you need to stop deluding yourself and face the lies that are keeping you stuck in a relationship that doesn't serve you. Once you bring these lies into the light, you will see how changing your attitude, your actions, and your outlook constitutes the one and only chance you have to make things better or get yourself out of the mess and move on.

♦◊♦

Here are the five lies we tell ourselves when we're stuck in a dysfunctional relationship.

1. I'm in control. This is the lie we tell ourselves that starts the dysfunctional cycle, because it's based on a dangerous and unsupportable relationship dynamic—assuming responsibility for managing your partner's emotions. I'm not talking about showing your partner how much you care or doing sensible or sweet things to foster harmony and affection. I'm talking about walking on eggshells and dancing on broken glass, watching your every move and editing your every word to prevent or forestall conflict. That's not control. It's letting fear control you. If your partner tends to be volatile, and you're keeping the peace with techniques, tricks, and tactics such as withholding information, sugar-coating, or simply suppressing your real feelings, while burning inside with shame, resentment, and the need to be vindicated, you're not being proactive—or helpful. You're placing your partner in the driver's seat, while sniping from the back, and everything you're doing is a reaction to the real or perceived threat of a fight. This reactive stance limits your range of behavioral options and confines you to a cramped box of your own making. You don't control a situation—or a relationship—by withdrawing from it. You can only control it, or share control, if you're present. Ironically, your efforts to avoid conflict by staying in the box often end up setting off the bombs instead of defusing them, as your discontent and unmet needs leak out in the form of passive-aggressive goading. The only way to take control is to stand up for yourself and express your true feelings. Your partner may not like the real you, but you can never be happy in a relationship if you don't like yourself because you can't be real.

2. My coping mechanisms are healthy. Really. There was a thing I did whenever my ex-wife was really getting to me, whenever I felt sick about what I was experiencing or my anger approached the level of a core meltdown. I would place my hand behind my back so she couldn't see it and clench my fist repeatedly, digging my nails into my flesh, as if I was trying to smash some small creature that I'd trapped inside my palm. I thought this reaction—this nervous tic—was normal, a release valve I used to let off steam and avoid the dangerous heat of conflict. But it was my body calling bullshit on my mind's delusional fantasy of my superhuman tolerance for emotional pain. I would also try to use mind over matter, saying to myself, "I can't take this anymore. But I can. And I will." The ultimate exercise in wishful thinking. Some of us blink. Some of us shudder. Some of us inhale sharply. Some of us start backing away and saying I'm sorry. And some of us reopen old wounds in the hope that causing our partner pain will get our partner to stop hurting us. That may work in a boxing ring, but a relationship is not a contest that the victor wins with a knockout blow. Any stifling of your true feelings to protect your partner's feelings or preserve a tenuous peace is ultimately unhealthy, not only because it causes you to suffer intense emotional damage, but also because it's unsustainable, as that damage is cumulative and builds to the point where the only way you can recover is to leave.

3. I love my partner. I'm sorry, but you don't. I know you don't believe me, because this is a tough pill to swallow. Almost as tough as #4 below. And it says something unflattering about you. But sacrificing your principles, your dreams of happiness, your self-respect, your dignity, your soul magic for another person—that isn't love. It's masochistic need-fulfillment—the need being yours to prove that your love can mend and heal a broken person, that your endless patience and tolerance and understanding can miraculously engender those same qualities in another, and that your superior reserves of warmth, compassion, and generosity can never be depleted. Chances are, your partner may be the type who demands proofs of love from you. "If you loved me, you would ..." But you're the one chasing the holy grail, indulging in the futile quest for proof that your love is enough to save someone, to make a shattered person whole again, to shape and polish a diamond to its highest purpose of shining light instead of acknowledging its ability to slice through bone. True love looks to confirm your own vulnerability, humility, and flawed humanity through supportive interaction with another, while what I'll call ego love appeals to your pride and looks to confirm your superior emotional stability and the power of your healing gifts.

4. My partner loves me. Bite it. Bite this bullet now and get over the idea that your dysfunctional dance partner loves you. If you're suffering abuse, it's surely not love and you should leave immediately. If it's not abuse but you're constantly miserable and eternally hopeful, you need to get real and stop using this lie as your crutch to limp through the horrid. Your partner may be capable of loving you, may even hold great love for you in the heart, but that love is blocked and absent from the day to day expression, and it doesn't inform the actions that influence the flow and feel of the time you spend together. Your interactions are not love actions but survival actions, as both of you struggle to stay alive, the way vampires fly through the night in search of fresh blood. Your partner may love the feeling of your capitulation, of his teeth sinking deep into your neck, or your subsuming yourself to her demands and mood swings. But your partner doesn't love you—only what you provide, and only as long as you provide it. I love the buzz I get after having a few drinks, but I can't love the booze itself. If it stopped getting me buzzed, I'd abandon it. Your partner loves the payoff of controlling you, and you take your cut in self-righteousness and resentment. The bottom line is when you love someone, you take accountability. You carefully examine your own contribution. And you don't mistake companionship, security, affection, sex, or the twisted intimacy of hand-to-hand combat for the commitment, courage, and covenant of true love.

5. It's a relationship. This is the mother of all lies that is built on all the others. It's definitely not a relationship. In *Co-Narcissism: How We Accommodate to Narcissistic Parents*, Alan Rappoport, Ph.D. wrote:

> *All of us are narcissistic, and co-narcissistic, to varying degrees. When our self-esteem varies in relation to how others think and feel about us, we are experiencing a narcissistic vulnerability. When we feel guilty or anxious because we fear that we are not meeting someone else's needs or expectations, we are being co-narcissistic. These ordinary experiences are problematic the more they interfere with our ability to be successful and enjoy our lives ....*

> *One of the critical aspects of the interpersonal situation when one person is either narcissistic or co-narcissistic is that it is not, in an important sense, a relationship. I define a relationship as an interpersonal in which each person is able to consider and act on his or her own needs,*

experience, and point of view, as well as being able to consider and respond to the experience of the other person. Both people are important to each person. In a narcissistic encounter, there is, psychologically, only one person present. The co-narcissist disappears for both people, and only the narcissistic person's experience is important ....

The key ... for most people who suffer from the narcissistic/co-narcissistic dilemma, [is] to experience a relationship in which neither person has to sacrifice himself for the other, and each can appreciate what the other has to offer.

If you're satisfying your partner's needs at the expense of your own, or vice versa, it's not a relationship of equals. And a relationship of equals is the only type of soil in which supportive, nurturing love—the kind of love a couple can grow into forever—can flourish.

The choice is yours. You can keep lying to yourself ...

Or you can reap the benefits of facing the truth.

The 3 Big Lies Abusers Rely On

Why do survivors stay in abusive relationships? Abusers use three lies to keep them from leaving.

———

People always ask why survivors of intimate partner violence and abuse stay with their abusers. "Why would anyone put up with that? Why don't they just leave?" Despite the resources listing the reasons people don't leave and pointing out the perils of departure, those who have not personally experienced abuse or seen it happen to someone close to them have tremendous difficulty wrapping their minds around how anyone "with a right mind" could get sucked into an abusive relationship, much less end up trapped in one, and eventually become a "victim" like the ones described in the articles that explain why people stay.

We tend to ignore problems we don't understand, but intimate partner violence and abuse, which not only damage (and sometimes end) lives but also set up a vicious and destructive multi-generational cycle cannot be ignored. The curtain must be pulled back to give people on the outside an inside view and enable them to recognize, respond to, and prevent this devastatingly harmful behavior.

Having lived through an emotionally abusive relationship myself, and lived in denial about it while it was happening, I'm in a position to help the skeptics and disbelievers see what really happens to abused partners and to unmask the mysterious power that keeps them in their abuser's thrall. While many factors are involved, I've boiled it down to three big lies that abusers rely on to keep their partners bound in the relationship. Each lie on its own has a crippling effect, but combined with one another, they paralyze the abused partner and make it impossible, without help, to escape the relationship.

◆◊◆

1.You're responsible for your partner's anger. This is how it begins. The abuser gets angry and expresses that anger through emotional or physical abuse. He (or she) presents the anger and the abuse that accompanies it as a normal, justifiable response to something the abused partner said or did, instead of an inappropriate reaction reflecting the abuser's lack of self-control and respect for boundaries. The abused partner believes this lie, assumes responsibility, apologizes (even though he or she is the one who was hurt), and determines to avoid the triggering behavior in the future, thus cutting him or herself off from healthy behavior, such as drawing a boundary or standing up for his or her own rights in the relationship. The lie puts the abused partner on the defensive, causes intense self-monitoring and second-guessing, and places the abused partner in the role of the hurter instead of the hurt one.

2. You're responsible for your partner's happiness. This lie plays on the abused partner's natural, healthy desire to please his or her mate, and it's why people-pleasers are prone to getting caught in abusive relationships. The abuser falsely empowers the abused partner by placing him or her in charge of the abuser's happiness and mental state, when in fact the guilt the abused partner feels over displeasing the abuser disempowers the abused partner and neutralizes his or her ability to take corrective action and stop the abuse. We are never responsible for another person's happiness, but the abused partner's belief that he or she is responsible is the nasty barb on abusive love's arrow: setting a boundary or leaving is seen not as an act of self-care or self-preservation but as a hostile, malicious act intended to cause the abuser misery. In addition, since we all hate to fail at anything, the abused partner keeps trying, even though the abuser can never sustain happiness.

3. You're responsible for fixing the relationship. Modern-day couples counseling encourages partners to see nearly everything that happens in a relationship as a relationship problem. How many articles and books tell you to hear your partner, to reflect back and validate, to join your partner in his or her pain before working on healing? It's natural, then, for an abused partner to view abuse in that context—a two-way street, a two-partner problem, and a shared responsibility to fix. But abuse is always a one-partner behavior pattern, and when it gets physical, it's also a crime. Regardless of whether an abused partner tolerates, triggers, or enables it, abuse is a behavior that must cease and that only the abuser is capable of ceasing. Unfortunately, many counselors lack the training or the strength to call a spade a spade when working with couples, especially if the abuse is only emotional and particularly if the abused partner expresses the desire to salvage the relationship.

I hope that calling out these three big lies helps people who are fortunate enough never to have experienced an abusive relationship to understand what abused partners go through as they fall down the rabbit hole, and why it becomes so vexingly difficult to climb back up again. If you believe your behavior makes the person you love angry and you feel obligated to make that person happy, you will try your damnedest—to the point of sacrificing yourself—to fix the problem and restore harmony and peace. You think you're taking the high road and being the bigger person. You think you're being kind and forgiving. You think you have the answers. The only answer to abuse is to walk away from it. But these lies obscure that answer so effectively that while you wish it was a possibility, you cross it off as an option. Having preyed on your vulnerability, the abuser now relies on your inability to leave to continue the torture, until you get enough help and support to make your escape.

Why We Stay With People Who Hurt Us

Healthy relationships involve compromise. But these three trades keep us bound in dysfunction.

———

When we remain in an unhealthy relationship, we believe we are waiting for our partner to change. In truth, we are waiting for ourselves to change, a process that often takes longer than we expect.

- Thomas G. Fiffer

———

Fifteen years.

Twenty-three years.

Thirty-one years.

These are not jail sentences—though they surely felt like time served in a dark, lonely, and dangerous place. No, these are the durations of three dysfunctional marriages— mine, a friend's, another friend's—in which we suffered insult and injury. Our partners felt trapped in misery, too— at least that's what they were always telling us—yet we clung with the ferocity of a wild animal tearing apart a piece of meat, held on with the life-sustaining grip of a rock climber, and refused to leave with the bull-like stubbornness of a child. We weren't making our partners happy, enabling growth, or building a secure future together. But we were determined to stay the course, complete the journey, push through the pain, and arrive at a place of peace and contentment, even if it killed us.

Books well worth reading have been written about co-dependent relationships, and the Stockholm Syndrome has been thoroughly explored. Survivors of abusive relationships have also cataloged some of the reasons they stayed—among them financial security, feelings of unworthiness fueled by their partner's disparagement, the savior complex, and the delusional state caused by wanting to believe their partners' endless apologies and promises to change. But I like to simplify things. So to spare you from studying clinical psychology, gobbling up self-help books filled with anecdotes about Bob and Sarah and Sam and Julie, and becoming an expert on the personality disorders listed in the DSM-V, here are what I see as three trades we make when we choose to stay with a partner who hurts us.

◆◇◆

1. We trade need for love. Need is primitive and elemental and immensely powerful. Need frequently overrules judgment. Our body informs us of basic physical needs—hunger, thirst, sexual release—and of pressing emergencies, such as air if we're suffocating or the need to evacuate our bowels. Emotional needs are more abstract—empathy, appreciation, fulfillment, human interaction—but manifest themselves in tangible presences such as an understanding partner, an appreciative boss, a rewarding job, and an active social life. The problem arises when we enter a relationship that meets one or more of our basic emotional needs but is not love-based. A partner can be empathic to our private pain, then turn and use our vulnerability against us. A boss can show appreciation for a job well done and publicly humiliate us when we fail. A friend can be a constant presence in our lives and a constant source of negativity. And a partner can be a phenomenal sexual match but a dreadful emotional companion. When we experience real love, we feel a sense of relaxation and peace that goes much deeper than the satisfaction of having our needs met. Love is a commitment that calls on us to meet a partner's needs and to do the work—on ourselves as well as with our partners—to form a healthy, lasting, and elastic bond. Trading need for love is unfair, because while we may get some or many of our needs met, we are missing out on the immeasurable joy of a loving relationship.

♦◊♦

2. We trade attachment for love. Setting aside the tremendous social pressure we experience to partner up and the stigma still attached to remaining single (not to mention childless), attachment is also a basic human need. Many animals live in packs or herds for safety, and on the social level the human animal has its own versions of these in tribes, cliques, organizations, and other groups. The basic human unit is the family, and the core of the family is the two-person couple. Attachment feels secure by its very nature, because being alone feels the opposite—lonely, insecure, and desperate. If we transform loneliness into solitude, we can find strength in independence, self-reliance, and resilience, but most people crave the feelings of emotional and physical security that being with a partner generates. The problem arises when we choose an unsafe partner, a person with a desire or need to harm us for his or her own self-soothing, a person who puts his or her needs before our best interests, a person who relies on attachment to us to indulge in unhealthy behavior. Real love is mutually supportive, unselfish, and never, ever hurtful. Trading love attachment for love is unfair, because we inhabit the shell of a loving relationship and hide behind a mask of happiness, while inside, there is emptiness. And by appearing to the world as happily partnered, we preclude other, more rewarding opportunities.

◆◇◆

3. We trade love of another for self-love. Our love for another, or another's love for us, no matter how powerful, cannot on its own sustain a healthy relationship. If we love another to the exclusion of self-love, we set ourselves up for a lifetime of disrespect. The statement that someone can only love you as much as you love yourself is true, because self-love sets the standard for what we will tolerate. Partners in dysfunctional relationships will often say, "I gave you everything" or "I sacrificed my life for you." When we give in ways that are hurtful to ourselves, we grow resentful, and we erode the self that our partner may have loved to begin with. We also allow a double standard and open ourselves up to mistreatment. Loving a partner generously, unreservedly, and wholeheartedly feels great and helps us feel good about ourselves, unless that person takes advantage of our devotion to act selfishly and disrespectfully, knowing that we will suck it up. And no matter how much love someone pours into our well, or vice versa, without self-love it can never be filled. Trading self-love for the love of another is unfair, because it offers a false sense of wholeness and enables us to avoid the critical work of coming to terms with and accepting who we are, faults and all.

Another reason people stay in hurtful relationships is our belief in what we call "unconditional love." People often ask what unconditional love means, unsure whether we still have to love someone if they hurt us because we can't attach conditions to love—such as refusing to tolerate abuse. Love is by definition an unconditional emotion, and love exists when love is mutual—when both partners treat each other in a truly loving fashion based on the core behaviors of kindness, respect, and generosity. When this happens, each partner gives without resentment, without keeping score, and without a second thought—unconditionally. It is when behavior in a relationship becomes conditional, when we start to hear, "If you loved me, you would … " that the relationship is no longer based on love but on transactional exchange. Love is always unconditional. When it's conditional, it is not love.

Now that you know how unfair these trades can be, you can think carefully before you make them.

7 Ugly Reasons We Cling When We Should Leave

Why do we hold out in horrible relationships? Here are 7 ugly ties that bind.

———

Everything depends upon courage: Without the ability to say 'no' your 'yes' means nothing.
- Rabbi David Wolpe

———

This morning I checked out some articles on why people stay in sucky relationships. My research rounded up the usual suspects. Topping the lists were fear of loneliness and guilt of hurting your partner along with hoping things will improve, and in the case of marriages, kids and money. I also noticed that most of these articles were not widely circulated, and that got me thinking: If these pieces didn't resonate, maybe they weren't identifying the real reasons we stay. Maybe fear and guilt, fantasy and delusion, kids and money are the stories we stick to, the surface adhesives, but not the true force behind the gravity of inertia. So I tried an experiment. I paralleled each of the seven deadly sins with a reason for staying, and I was surprised by my revelations. You may be, too.

♦◊♦

1. Lust. This first one is obvious. The sex is phenomenal. The relationship isn't. You fight like cats and dogs every day and f**k like bunnies every night. Angry sex can be hot, and you can work out a lot of nastiness by doing the nasty. Plus, mind-blowing, body-shuddering orgasms cover a multitude of sins. But there's no substitute for sex that flows naturally from love and consummates—rather than tries to concoct—emotional intimacy. If you've never experienced this deep, intense bonding, you don't know what you're missing, and you're staying for chemistry and compatibility, not true connection. The inability to come together with words speaks volumes about your relationship.

2. Gluttony. It's not about food, but it is about consumption. If you're a glutton, you stay because you're getting all your needs met while not meeting your partner's, and you're consuming all the energy and resources in the relationship. This lopsided dynamic is a sweet deal for the glutton and attracts many people whose personality disorders feed on it to thrive. But gluttony sucks big time for the giver, who's constantly being depleted. A rare glutton who loves his or her partner will either work to restore balance or gracefully step away and stop taking, but most remain at the trough as long as they can. Meanwhile, givers delude themselves that one more morsel will be enough, not realizing it's their depletion itself that gives the glutton pleasure.

3. Greed. Greed follows gluttony, but it's less about money and more about conquest. You got someone. That person is yours, and you're not going to let go, even if holding on is unhealthy and will eventually destroy you. Greed-based relationships center on ownership and control and the greedy partner's fear of loss and sense of entitlement. Loss of any kind is terrifying, and losing your partner—even if that person is a source of pain and torment—is unbearable. The more a healthy person asserts power and independent rights, the more a greedy person clamps down on the insurrection. If you're the rebel, you fear punishment, because greedy partners have a scorched earth policy. They'd rather see you dead than with someone else.

4. Sloth. Sometimes, you're just too lazy to make a change. You're set in your habits, and life is predictable, even if it's predictably unhappy. Change is risky—you could end up worse off. So you rationalize: I may not be joyously fulfilled, but little is expected of me, and I don't expect much of my partner, which enables us both to avoid disappointment. Sloth is perhaps the saddest of reasons. The only growth in a sloth-based relationship is the weeds overtaking your field of dreams, the vines twisting around and strangling your tree of life, as the crumbling foundation you've built with your partner sinks and settles into the ground.

5. Wrath. Wrath keeps you bound in misery in two ways. First, anger can substitute for intimacy. I've written about this in "Why Couples Fight: The Real Cause of Conflict." But the wrath that enables you to eviscerate your partner every day and leave Prometheus to grow a new liver every night is the wrath fueled by your hatred of your partner and your desire for revenge over how you feel you've been treated. You're staying to exact punishment, to pursue your pound of flesh. Punishment is never appropriate between adults (except in the criminal justice system), but that doesn't stop wrathful partners from inflicting pain they see as deserved. Often, the recipient accepts the punishment as penance, failing to see there is no chance of redemption.

6. Envy. Envy is "resentful longing" aroused by someone else's accomplishments or good fortune. The envious partner wants what he or she believes other "happy" couples have and will twist a counterpart in knots to get it. "You're a complete failure, a poor excuse for a husband—or wife. We should have …" and the list is endless. When you're envious, you'd rather harangue a partner into providing your happiness than make the effort to create it yourself. You're also aware on some level that another partner might not tolerate your ranting, so you keep firing arrows where they've already hit. The partner being pierced experiences shame and begins to buy into being responsible for your plight, and the barbed hook is set.

7. Pride. Some people take pride in being coupled or fear the opposite—feeling shamefully incomplete if they are not. But the pride that keeps partners mired in misery takes two familiar forms. One is the pride of relationship longevity: "I've made it this far, and I'm not giving up now," a stance that ignores sunk costs and the need to shear the chain of the anchor. The other is the pride of the animal trainer: "I've worked hard to train my monkey to perform, to behave obediently, to come when I call, to beg beseechingly when I dangle a treat, to submit humbly to the lash of my bullwhip." The irony here is that the trained-monkey partner takes equal pride in being a doormat, in meeting any and every unreasonable request just to keep receiving the crumbs.

It you find yourself clinging for any of these reasons, it's time for a partnerectomy, a clean cut that sets you both free from each other, severs the unhealthy entanglement, and opens up possibilities for happiness and growth.

Why Couples Fight: The Real Cause of Conflict

All couples disagree, most argue, and some slug it out with words day after day. Learn the real source of discord, how it escalates to conflict, and how to stop it from derailing your relationship.

———

"You never understand me, John. You never know what I want. I tell you, but you don't listen. It's always all about you. You're just an insensitive jerk."

♦◊♦

"Jane, I bust my butt every day for you. And you never appreciate it. You're always on my case, criticizing me, telling me I don't do enough, make enough, making me feel inadequate, comparing me to our friends."

♦◊♦

"You know, John, without me you'd be nothing. I'm the best thing that ever happened to you. You'll never find a woman like me, and once you realize that, maybe you'll start treating me better."

"Look, Jane, what do you want me to do? I've apologized a hundred times already. You bring up these old hurts, every time you're upset with me. You sound like a broken record. I said I was sorry. Now can't we be done with it?"

It's sooooo aggravating. John and Jane are both reasonably, maybe even super-intelligent people. They love each other. They may parent together. And yet they can't seem to resolve a disagreement, or even agree to disagree and move on? Why? Because they're both defending untenable positions that don't address the underlying issues plaguing their relationship. These issues hide below the surface and, like a drop of acid added to water, convert disagreement into conflict. "But wait!" John says. "That's NOT the problem. The problem is, I'm right and Jane's is wrong. She never listens." "If only John would understand," Jane counters. "If only I could convince him." Think again. **They're both wrong**— not necessarily in logical terms—but in their approach to the conflict and the behavior patterns they've developed to deal with it. If John and Jane sound familiar to you, read on.

♦◊♦

When I first started seeing my therapist and complaining about the things my ex-wife and I fought about, he shared some electrifying words with me that changed my entire understanding of the conflict in my marriage. He said, **"Pay no attention to the content."** My first reaction was outrage. "What? Don't pay attention to what I'm hearing? But she said . . ." And you're probably thinking the same thing. "I'm supposed to ignore my partner's outrageous statements, lies or misrepresentations, insults and inaccuracies, the 'you never' and 'you always' sentences that spell the death of healthy communication? Yes, I'm telling you to **ignore the content,** the words themselves, as well as the situation or issue that precipitated the argument. Because **none of that is important**, and none of it is relevant to what's actually happening. Here's why. When partners engage in endless, unresolvable conflict, the conflict is about **feelings**, not what triggered those feelings. This truth becomes clear after a while, because as the relationship progresses, more and more incidents trigger the same feelings, and things that didn't incite a reaction in earlier days become flash points for bitter fights and even violent rage. And when rage sets in, there's no hope for resolution.

The real cause of conflict is lost intimacy.

The feelings that underlie endless conflict are generally hurt, disappointment, betrayal, deprivation, abandonment, or loneliness, or wrapped into a bundle—not feeling loved. When we're thirsty we go for our favorite drink, and if it's not available, we'll take water. If we're stuck in the desert, we're grateful for the drops of moisture found inside a cactus, and if we're desperate, we'll drink our own urine to stay alive. When we're thirsty for love, we go for our favorite source of love, our partner. But if our partner is unavailable for emotional or sexual intimacy, we look for a substitute. Not a substitute partner—though that may eventually occur if things get dire. A substitute for intimacy. And what does a better job of getting us eye to eye and toe to toe, right in each other's faces, and gives us an opportunity to show just how intimately we know our partner, than a fight? We become aroused, passionate. Things get hot. And silence, if it's plaguing the relationship in the form of withholding, is broken as words—cruel and insensitive ones perhaps—but still, words, are finally exchanged. Put another way, a fish will swim away from a hook, because a hook means pain and possibly death. But bait? Bait means food. And food means life, so bait is tempting. So one partner baits the other—with a statement, often hostile, that is difficult to ignore. The other partner reacts, and the fight is on. Suddenly, you're thrashing wildly as you're being reeled in again to the endless argument. It is not always one partner who does the baiting, because both crave intimacy and each is just as llkely to start a conflict, consciously or not, to achieve a semblance of closeness.

It's the feelings, stupid.

When a young child is upset, the child often blubbers and babbles. Words don't form, because the brain is overloaded with emotion and the cognitive circuits are fried. But we understand instantly from tone and expression that the child is in distress. The same thing happens with the endless argument, only it occurs between adults. One partner feels hurt, disappointed, betrayed, deprived, abandoned, lonely, or all of the above, and the intensity of these painful feelings overloads the parts of the brain that manage communication. It's the way you feel when you just want to scream. In addition, while the other partner's action or inaction may have triggered these painful feelings, they often relate to wounds from the first one's past relationships or childhood that the other neither caused nor is capable of healing. Unable to identify the source of the upset, the angry partner focuses on his or her mate as the target and relieves the intense emotional discomfort by blaming him or her for something—anything—convenient. It doesn't matter that the couple may have been over this particular issue time and time again. The issue is not the point; it's a place holder for emotions. The words are meaningless, but the emotions are real. If you focus on the words, you grow intensely frustrated with your partner's irrational, non-constructive behavior of confronting you with an issue you thought you had resolved. Your reaction feeds the cycle of the endless argument, because no logical counter you can offer will lessen the pain your partner is experiencing. When is the last time an argument ever changed a feeling?

Hurt is inevitable; it's how we handle it.

Feelings of hurt, disappointment, betrayal, deprivation, and abandonment make intimacy impossible, because they block trust. Once we realize our partner is capable of hurting us deeply—a natural condition of intimacy—we become afraid it will happen again. We put up walls, grow defensive and aloof, distance ourselves from our partners to protect our egos and our feelings, and soon enough loneliness sets in. Real intimacy requires risk, and most partners are risk averse in relationships, especially those who suffered deep hurts in previous partnerships or in childhood. It is a truth universally acknowledged that at some time or another, your partner will hurt you. This is a fact of being in relationships. The key to healthy relationships is how we handle being hurt, along with recognizing whether the pain being caused is intentional or not. It hurts just as much if it isn't intentional, but it's easier to forgive if it isn't. It may, however, not be easier to correct, because if your partner isn't aware he or she is hurting you, that awareness must precede corrective action. If your partner is aware of hurting you and intentionally continues, it's not a relationship but an abusive situation, and you would serve yourself well by seeking counseling as to why you're still in it. If you love each other and want to stop fighting, you need to realize that when we feel hurt, being right, being vindicated, soothes it, even if being right comes at the expense and pain of our partner, someone we love. That's why insisting on being right is wrong, and being right is not an inalienable right but an alienating behavior.

The endless argument is so much easier to start than a dialogue about the lack of trust or the feelings that underlie it that partners fall into the destructive routine of fighting to replace the intimacy they have lost and would like to regain. Breaking your dependence on fighting to achieve intimacy is crucial to restoring the health of your relationship.

Ignore the content and stop the fight.

This simple trick for contributing partners helps you ignore the content and break the devastating cycle of the endless argument. First, strip away the words. Listen to the tone, the pitch, the rhythm of your partner's voice, humming quietly along with it to block out the actual words being spoken. When your partner is done speaking, say something like, "You know, that's really terrible, and I'd like to help. Can you tell me in one word what emotion you're feeling right now?" Often the answer will be, "anger." If it is, you can follow with, "Can you identify in one or two words the source of your anger?" Your partner is likely to say this is you. Here's where you work your magic. Help your partner understand that **a person can't be the cause of anger or any other emotion**, that **emotions such as anger are our reactions to actions or words**. "OK, so I'm angry with what you said (or did)."

Now, here's the hard part—**accept your partner's anger**. Accept that it exists and is real. Then, explain to your partner that **anger is a secondary emotion**, a feeling that floods us after we experience primary emotions such as hurt, fear, rejection, or humiliation. Ask your partner if he or she can identify the feeling that came just before the anger. If, for example, it's hurt, you can say, "I'm sorry you feel hurt. Let's talk about where that feeling is coming from." By taking charge and shifting the dynamic, you begin to guide your partner away from the quick fix of relieving pain by blaming you and towards the pain's true source. The response you encounter may be, "Well, I feel hurt whenever you talk to your mother on the phone," or "Every time you come home late I feel abandoned." If you can slip out from under feeling blamed and responsible for your partner's feelings, you can engage in a more constructive dialogue focused on intent. A statement such as, "I didn't intend to hurt you by calling my mother or coming home late" joins the two of you in an effort to avoid the hurt and improve the relationship. This can be followed with, "How can we handle this situation going forward to avoid your feeling hurt?"

Functional communication is intimate and sexy.

Earlier, I explained how arguing serves as a substitute for intimacy. When partners can't connect in a healthy way, when the thrill of romance and the easy flow of love are gone, they often resort to fighting to restore a measure of closeness. And fighting, in its own way, can be sexy, especially if the kiss and make up part follows. But in truth, there's nothing closer and more intimate than being in complete agreement with your partner, being in sync and on the same page, and there's nothing sexier than the security of knowing you can always talk to your partner about anything and not get blindsided, ambushed, or slammed. Lines connect at a point, and for partners to connect, there must be a point of connection—a shared perception, perspective, principle, or goal. This can be as simple as the desire for peace and harmony in the home and the relationship, and the commitment to work to make that a reality.

♦◊♦

Here are some examples of functional communication around typical issues that dysfunctional couples fight about in the endless argument.

> *"I've been putting it off and need to call my mother about dinner on Sunday. It's important to me that we go, but I know you have feelings about it. Would you like to talk about it so we can get on the same page before I call?"*

This statement acknowledges that your partner has an issue with seeing your family or your relationship with your mother and offers a conciliatory gesture in advance of an action you are aware could be triggering.

"When you didn't call me all day today from work, I felt really lonely. I'm sure you were busy, and I understand. Now that you're home, maybe we can relax and catch up, talk a little about my day —and yours?"

This statement establishes hurt feelings then quickly transforms them into a request for intimacy. Instead of closing the door with an attack, it opens the door for an apology that your partner knows will be accepted and creates an opportunity for restoring connection and trust.

♦◊♦

"When you don't discipline Dylan and make me the heavy, I feel like the rug's been pulled out from under me. I know we both disapprove of his behavior, and we both want him to change it, but we'll be stronger as parents and he'll be better off, too, if we can support each other when it comes to discipline."

This statement expresses the feeling of abandonment while at the same time extending a bridge to your partner on the issue of discipline. It also suggests a way forward that doesn't blame the child's behavior on the more indulgent parent.

You may not think of these suggested exchanges as the best way to get your partner into the bedroom, but they sure beat a fight that ends up with only one of you in the bed and the other on the couch.

A Theory on the Role of Love in Abuse

Both abusers and victims claim they love and are loved by their partners. But what does love have to do with abuse?

———

One of the greatest sources of confusion about abusive relationships for people who have never been in one is how abusers can claim to love their victims while treating them so horribly, and how, in turn, victims cite loving their abusive partners as a reason for staying. If love is patient, kind, understanding, and compassionate—and surely love is not dismissive, mean, contemptuous, and violent—then where is the love in abuse?

I'm not a psychologist, nor am I an expert on abuse. But having lived through an emotionally abusive relationship and gone through therapy to understand it, I come to the question from more than a distanced, intellectual or clinical perspective. And in exploring my feelings, as well as my thoughts, about intimate partner abuse, I have reached some conclusions I believe are worth sharing.

Let's start with a truth that can be universally acknowledged. Both partners come to any intimate relationship seeking love, or more accurately, what to them feels like love. Understanding that something can feel like love but not be love is a crucial distinction. For the abusive partner, what feels like love is complete, unconditional acceptance. For the abused partner, what feels like love is special treatment—being the sole and intense focus of another's attention, warmth, and desire. The reasons for the abusive partner's need for acceptance and the abused partner's need for special treatment (which interestingly are more similar than different) are critical, but they belong in a different discussion of causality. For now, keep in mind that each partner brings to the relationship a behavior that makes the other one feel loved, and each partner has a history of trading that behavior to gain the love feeling—acceptance to gain special attention, or special attention to gain acceptance.

In the beginning, things are happy, often deliriously so. Critical mutual needs are—finally—met. This one seems to be the one. The abusive partner turns on the charm to gain acceptance, lavishing attention, warmth, and desire on the other during the courtship period, which the soon-to-be-abused partner soaks up as (feeling like) love. In return, the other partner ignores (accepts) serious red flags that indicate problems are likely down the road. The soon-to-be-abused partner is effectively blind to these signals, because the need for special treatment in the now overwhelms uncertainty about the future. But after a while, two major shifts occur. First, the special treatment diminishes, partly because it is unsustainable but also because doubt tortures the abuser's mind. The abuser needs to know that the love isn't contingent on the special treatment. But as the special treatment fades, so does the other partner's acceptance. And so the abuse begins, as the abuser starts demanding proofs of acceptance which are presented as proofs of love.

Will you still love me if I ignore you?
Will you still love me if I insult you?
Will you still love me if I accuse you?
Will you still love me if I betray you?
Will you still love me if I make you feel worthless?
Will you still love me if I threaten you?
Will you still love me if I hit you?
Will you still love me if I use your vulnerability against you?
Will you still love me if I hurt you in ways you never imagined?

You'd think the abused partner would say no to all of these questions, but here's the kicker: the special treatment the abused partner craves—the apologies, the love notes, the flowers, the dinners, the gifts, the promises, the make-up sex—follows and becomes intimately linked to each instance of hurt. The abused partner begins trading acceptance of abuse (instead of acceptance of his or her partner) for special treatment, and asks only one question: "Will the special treatment return if I tolerate and forgive this?" Thus begins the cycle.

♦◊♦

At first, the abused partner doesn't perceive the onset of a cycle but a need for more effort to make the relationship work. Craving the special treatment that, for him or her, feels like love, the abused partner decides that a little suffering is worth it to be with a person, perhaps the only person they've ever found, who gives them the love feeling. But the stakes in the cycle get higher and higher. As the abuser's need for acceptance escalates, so does the intensity of the abuse, and the special treatment that follows the abuse also ratchets up to make up for greater and greater emotional and/or physical harm, making the "payoff" greater for the abused partner. The couple quickly becomes trapped in a toxic cycle, in which an incident of abuse is the necessary catalyst to trigger the flow of unsustainable special treatment. This may result in the abused partner subconsciously triggering the abuser, even though the abused partner is consciously walking on eggshells and trying to avoid those triggers. No, the abused partner is never asking for—and never deserves —abuse, but he or she may very well be engaging in behavior (even if it is just tolerating abuse) that sustains the cycle. To understand this twisted dynamic, an outside observer has to look at both parts of the cycle and see it as a whole—hurtful act followed by loving act—rather than just looking at the hurtful acts and asking, "Why on earth would anyone put up with that?" and "Why on earth would anyone call that love?"

The abusive partner's need for complete, unconditional acceptance also explains his or her focus on details and demands for perfection. He flies off the handle if his shirt wasn't ironed properly or dinner isn't ready exactly on time, or she loses it when her partner comes home late or forgets the milk, because getting these things exactly right constitutes proof of acceptance and love and getting them wrong makes them feel unloved. But no matter how hard the abused partner tries, the abuser always manages to find fault.

In turn, instead of simply drawing a line and saying, "What I'm doing for you will have to be good enough," the abused partner tries harder and harder to satisfy the abuser, both to avoid the hurt that follows failure and, as significantly, in the hopes of receiving more of the special treatment that feels like love. The irony is that the special treatment rarely follows the perfect execution of the abuser's impossible demands but always follows an incident of abuse. Bam! This pattern dooms to failure the abused partner's efforts to obtain special treatment by meeting the abuser's expressed need for perfection, because it is the very failure to achieve that perfection that triggers the cycle that brings on the abuse and the subsequent special treatment by the abuser. The truth is, no amount of acceptance—or special treatment—can fill either partner's needs.Both partners suffer repeated pain and disappointment as they remain trapped in a sickening cycle of hurt and futility that, due to their misconceptions, both readily characterize as love. Each says to him or herself, "I've found the one who makes me feel loved … as long as I can handle the awful hurt that comes with it."

This theory (and I emphasize it is a theory that does not apply to every case) defines the cycle of abuse as the constant, repeated seeking of love—or more accurately, what feels like love—by both partners in a co-dependent manner. The abusive partner makes an impossible demand for unconditional acceptance, which the abused partner inevitably fails to meet. The abused partner also makes a less overt demand for special treatment, which the abuser is only capable of providing after an incident of abuse. Abuse occurs, followed by special treatment as a corrective. The cycle continues. It seems then, that the way to break the cycle is either for the relationship to end or for both partners to shift their definitions and practice of love. For the relationship to become healthy, both partners must understand that love is neither complete acceptance nor special treatment and not a continuous cycle of suffering followed by recompense but rather a complex combination of mutual respect, honesty, empathy and compassion, and commitment to communicate about and resolve problems in a loving and constructive way. This definition doesn't sound as romantic as unconditional acceptance or special treatment, and it involves a lot less drama, but it is the stuff of which successful, long-term relationships are made. Love without boundaries is not love at all; it is obsession where the end of getting one's unhealthy needs met justifies the means of destroying another person.

When Leaving Seems Impossible …

For partners stuck in dysfunctional relationships, here's a roadmap for getting out.

———

You know it's not right. You've always known it deep down, though it may have felt right, almost too right, at the beginning.

"He said I was the only one for him. He made me feel so special."

"She knew we were soul mates from day one."

Now you wish to God you'd never met this person, much less moved in, gotten married, or had children with someone who seems determined to make your life a living hell.

"My family told me to slow down, but he couldn't wait to get married."

"All her previous partners were a-holes. But I was different."

And now?

♦◊♦

"I'm not a masochist," you say. "I just got stuck in a tough situation. I was taught to stick it out, and I'm going to make the best of it."

I hear you. I was you. But hear me. Because here's the rub.

The first step to getting out of something that's killing you is to understand that you're in something that's killing you. That your emotional life is not immortal. That some things are unsustainable. That eventually, you'll collapse in a heap that doctors call a nervous breakdown. Either that, or you'll do something to your partner or yourself that you'll regret. Either way, you're looking at irreparable damage if you stay, but you've deluded yourself into believing you can take it. Just one more day. Just one more year. Wise up and check your damage-ometer, the kind that appears over the characters in your kids' video games. How many bars do you have left? Two, maybe only one? Your family's worried about you, but they don't want to interfere. Your friends won't say you look like shit to your face, but they talk about you after you leave. You're living a pretend life—happy on the outside, miserable within. Am I getting through yet?

Painful as it is, you can eventually become aware of what's actually happening in your relationship. You don't need my help for that. Just the kick I already gave. What's harder to grasp, and where assistance is helpful, are the flawed reasons that are keeping you imprisoned, the false belief that you cannot leave. I've identified four blocks that keep us chained in dysfunctional relationships. There may be more, but I consider these the four horsemen of the relationship apocalypse. Each centers around avoiding something our brains are wired to hate and fear, which is why it's so hard to see leaving as being in our ultimate best interest. Once we strip away the accumulated dirt and debris on these blocks, they reveal themselves as the means of our escape, the golden tickets we can hand over for a journey towards happiness and fulfillment. So here they are, along with a strategy to turn each one around and use it to your advantage. There's a phrase I'm fond of when people ask me how to travel from despair to joy when these two points seem so distant. "You have to bend the map," I say. And that's exactly what these strategies will do for you.

◆◇◆

1. Admitting failure. Let's face it. We hate to fail. I know I do. It feels shameful. Embarrassing. Humiliating. Sure, we're told it's OK to fail in business. Fail frequently. Fail up. Fail your way to the top. But when we fail in a relationship, especially more than one, we always wonder. Did I not try hard enough? Is there something wrong with me? Or the worst question: Am I not relationship material? We'd much rather say, "I'm struggling," than "I gave up," even when giving up means our salvation, even when there are no more boundaries left for our partner to overstep. The way around admitting failure? Shift your perspective. You're not admitting failure. You're acknowledging futility. There's no way you could have succeeded at this, no way anyone could. And the sooner you make the move to an environment where you can succeed, the faster your ascent will be.

2. Loss of sunk costs. Almost as bad as failure is the total loss of an investment—a wipeout—and particularly a costly one. We feel foolish. Stung. Stupid. And full of regret. If time is money, we keep throwing good years after bad (in my case, 15 years) with the hope that next year things will turn around, the stock will go up again, and the relationship will be right again—the way it was in those blissful early days. Only it never happens that way, because dysfunctional partners are like bottomless pits, and they keep demanding more. Even when you're tapped out, exhausted, depleted to the core, they kick you like a dray horse and add to the load. The way around sunk costs is to act like a shrewd investor and cut your losses without emotion. When the decision to leave becomes about your survival, not your partner's disappointment, hurt feelings, or nasty reaction, it's a simple calculation—you live or you die—instead of tangled morass of questioning and guilt.

3. Trading bad for worse. Sure, my situation sucks. But it could be worse, so I might as well stay. It's possible your partner has tried to convince you that the hell you're in is normal and that no one has it any different. That's a typical tactic of abuse. Combine this with our innate tendency to focus on the good things a partner offers (particularly the physical) and minimize or ignore the bad, and you end up believing that most people suffer similar tortures to yours. But think carefully about what you tell your friends or family—which is what you're telling yourself—and compare it to the truth. Chances are if you opened up about what was really going on, your friends and family would be horrified. They might even schedule an intervention. And you'd get confirmation that what you're experiencing isn't anywhere near normal. You'd learn that other people enjoy partnerships based on supportiveness and respect. The way around trading bad for worse is honesty. Take your veil off and see the world through new eyes.

4. Fear of loneliness. This is by far the toughest of the four blocks. No one wants to be alone. I stayed in a dysfunctional marriage for years partly for this reason. I was afraid I wouldn't ever find anyone else. We're designed to thrive on companionship, and healthy relationships (whether intimate or just friendly) play a key role in both physical health and longevity. Fear of loneliness is cold and paralyzing. It stops us from taking risks. It leads us to substitute being tolerated for being accepted, to settle for indifference instead of demanding respect, to mistake being wanted and needed for being loved. Combine this with a partner who constantly tells you no one else would want you, and you're frozen in a cave of ice. The way around fear of loneliness is pulling the future into the present and see that your worst fear has already come to pass. As Robin Williams said as Lance Clayton in World's Greatest Dad, "I used to think the worst thing in life is to end up all alone. It's not. The worst thing in life is ending up with people who make you feel all alone."

I hope these four strategies will help you bend your own maps and make the journey out of hurtful, destructive relationships. You deserve better, and you can have better. In relationship physics, the shortest distance between two points is not always a straight line, and happiness is actually much closer than you think.

5 Reasons It's So Hard to Leave Crazy

**You're in a place that makes no sense, and you can't find your way out.
It's called ... crazy.**

___

*Oh, crazy
For thinking that my love could hold you
I'm crazy for trying
And crazy for crying
And I'm crazy for loving you*

- Patsy Cline, *Crazy*

___

Some of us have traveled to—or through—the torturous twilight zone of living with a person who perceives the world differently (a polite euphemism for a disordered personality), and others have watched friends or family members disappear into the darkness—an alternate universe from which there is no evident means of escape. The entrance is through the wormhole (more on how we get sucked in to come in another article), and the exit is made invisible by a confluence of factors and an abundance of fog. Below are five reasons we fail to find our way out of dysfunction and back to the land of the healthy relationship.

◆◇◆

1. We love the person we want our partner to be—and believe he or she is capable of being. This is the fantastical wish-desire that keeps us trapped in dysfunctional relationships, often for long stretches of our life. We formed an image of our partner, usually in the early stages of courtship, only to discover later that the person we saw then has vanished or never actually existed. In some cases, dysfunctional partners assume appealing disguises to lure us, then later shed them once we're hooked. In others, we blindly project our own vision of perfection onto a partner (who, surprise, turns out to be human) and opt to live in delusion to avoid the disappointment of facing the truth. Either way, we remain eternally hopeful, latching on to the tiniest signs of change or improvement to indulge the fantasy that happiness is right around the bend. It's one thing to encourage a partner to grow and develop and to hold someone we love dearly to a high standard of behavior. It's entirely another to make it our life's mission—and sacrifice our own happiness—to "help" someone become a person he or she wasn't and will never be.

2. Our partner makes us think we're the crazy one. Call it what you want: mirroring, transference, turnabout, or psychological manipulation. In virtually every dysfunctional relationship, the primary (or the one I call controlling) dysfunctional partner tries to convince the other partner that he or she is the root cause of conflict and must get help to restore harmony. The truth is that both partners have roles in the dysfunctional drama. But the reason this tactic is so devastatingly effective is that the partner accused of being crazy actually believes the accuser and begins to dismantle his or her own psyche—not in the healthy way that opens the path to growth, but in the destructive way that leads to intense self-criticism. "If only I could give more. If only I could love better. If only I could be more supportive." This narrative of inadequacy eventually gets internalized, to the point where the partner doing the criticizing doesn't have to say a word. We do all their work for them.

3. Our partner accuses us of the things they're guilty of doing. What's the best way to prevent an enemy from finding your weaknesses? Distraction. In dysfunctional relationships, where truth becomes the ultimate enemy, this means shifting your partner's focus to his or own issues (real or imaginary) and away from yours. This tactic takes two forms. First, there is the flip, in which, for example, a partner who withholds attention and affection accuses you of doing the same, and blames his or her distance and unavailability on something you said or didn't say, or did or didn't do. "How can I be affectionate to someone who doesn't love me?" "What do you mean, I don't love you?" "Well, if you loved me, you wouldn't have spent an hour talking to your girlfriend on the phone." "But I hadn't spoken to her in two years, and you were busy playing your video game like you always do." Sound familiar? The other tactic is the pre-emptive strike. Your partner makes a mistake or does something hurtful, and before you can address it, accuses you of something

awful. You become so busy defending yourself that your partner's action gets set aside or ignored.

4. We think we can cure our partner. Are you a psychiatrist? A psychologist? A social worker? A nurse? What qualifications do you have to treat mental illness? It's likely your partner is using you as medicine instead of seeking appropriate professional help, draining your well and depleting your energy, relying on pushing you under water day after day to be able to stay afloat. Choose whichever metaphor you like; the unfortunate truth is you're being used, drained, or sunk. You've deluded yourself into believing that you—and only you—have the power to help your partner, and you've coupled this with the fear that if you stop helping, he or she will collapse or worse, die or take his or her own life. You don't dare remove your finger from the dyke. You may indeed have healing powers, but you can't heal someone who refuses healing. After a while it becomes clear—to everyone but you—that your strongest power is the one that weakens you the most, the power of self-sacrifice, the power to shrink yourself to nothing and pretend you are nobody to keep your partner's ego on life support.

5. We get off on feeling superior and sane. If you're stuck in a dysfunctional relationship, any good therapist you see will ask you two questions—two questions you don't want to answer. The first is, "What is your contribution?" and the second is, "What are you getting out of staying?" Your contribution is likely to be complex, and it may take you some to admit your own flaws, triggers, predispositions, and unhealthy behaviors. They may not be on the same scale as your partner's, but you are still participating in the dysfunctional dance. What you are getting out of staying will also differ from person to person, but one common payoff for people who stay with "crazy" partners is what I call the relativity benefit. You use your partner's dysfunctional behavior to reassure yourself that you're healthy and sane. This tends to occur in the latter part of the relationship cycle, in which you've gone from hoping your partner will become someone else to demonizing your partner for who he or she is. "I'm the sane one" gives you a free pass that enables you to justify a wide range of unhealthy behaviors and covers a multitude of sins. You become your own judge and jury, and because you've now discounted your partner's opinions, you no longer have to listen to them. I'm a believer in the grain of truth theory, which means there's a nugget somewhere in the dysfunctional partner's ravings. But once you indulge in the self-righteous self-justification that you hate so much in your partner, you begin to lose your moral authority.

So how do we leave? If only we could call Mr. Scott on our transponders and ask him to please beam us back up to normal. Ironically, we do often have to atomize our own personas before we can reassemble them into a healthy whole. The way out of a dysfunctional relationship is slow and painful. First, you have to step back. Detach yourself from the roles you and your partner play and look rationally at behavior between two people. Are you with a miserable, disrespectful person who happens to be your husband, boyfriend, girlfriend, or wife? If the answer is yes, start to recognize the patterns. Identify your role in them and separate it from your partner's. Determine to break the patterns by changing your behavior. This won't be easy, and you'll need to prepare yourself for unpleasant consequences—not just your partner's anger but the end of the relationship. Hold your ground and maintain your boundaries. Make the issue your partner's behavior, not his or her personality. Don't label, and don't judge or condemn. Keep the focus on yourself and your own emotional health. If you do the work on that exclusively, you'll eventually find yourself back home.

The 7-Day Relationship Detox Diet

Relationships suffering from cumulative damage can reach a tipping point that spells disaster. This 7-day prescription stops the poisoning and helps restore your relationship's health.

———

We do not realize that our lives are changing until they have already unalterably changed.

———

You know the scene in *The Simpsons Movie* when Homer dumps the silo of pig poop into Springfield's lake? The seemingly clean water starts to bubble green and black, a skull and crossbones appears on the surface, and Homer trembles as it speaks the word, "Evil." Homer's careless polluting pushes the lake past its toxic tipping point, marking Springfield for quarantine and destruction. Just seconds before, however, everything seemed OK. The lake looked normal. And it is this illusion of normalcy that makes the change so shocking and deadly.

We don't realize it—or not until it's too late—but relationships are like the lake. The winds are favorable and it's smooth sailing, and then suddenly—WHAM! Out of nowhere, the ship capsizes and a couple is in crisis. An affair prompted by crushing loneliness. A blow up with words one can never take back. Or the simple act of walking away. What the f**k just happened? The moment the event occurs is more than a moment. It is the sum total of a million moments in which things were silently going wrong, pain went unacknowledged, feelings were not expressed, truths were not told, and unseen damage was ravaging the fabric that binds the relationship. My first marriage limped along for 15 years before the wounds, which I knew were crippling, revealed themselves as mortal. My second, which I entered before healing fully, lasted just 24 months. Use whatever metaphor you like— a rope fraying, moths eating holes in cloth, termites eroding a house from within, or slow and steady poisoning —they all describe the cumulative damage that builds and builds and eventually breaks up most dysfunctional partnerships.

◆◇◆

To keep our bodies healthy, we exercise and diet, while our immune system does the rest of the work. Relationships are no different. They require constant maintenance and a healthy regime. This means consuming what's good for the relationship and avoiding what's not. It's the avoiding part I'm focusing on here. For each day of the week, I've identified a behavior to stop practicing, a belief to stop clinging to, a fantasy to stop indulging. Giving these things up isn't easy, but in one week you will begin to see measurable results. You'll feel happier, lighter, and more optimistic. Caveat: This won't work for everyone. Some relationships are too far gone to be helped, but many can be saved from death and dissolution. And everyone does this stuff in healthy relationships, too, just a lot less of it.

◆◇◆

Monday—Stop thinking things will get better by themselves. They won't. If entropy fixes anything, it's purely by accident. This is a convenient delusion, a hope-wish that absolves you of the uncomfortable responsibility to act. Be honest with yourself that your relationship is in trouble and acknowledge that serious work needs to be done. Share this realization with your partner. It could be the one thing you finally agree on.

Tuesday—Stop blaming everything on your partner. Sure, some things are your partner's fault. But some things are yours. If it's truly all one-sided, you might as well ditch the relationship. Why would you want to stay with someone who is 100% responsible for shattering your dreams? The truth is, self-righteousness is grossly unattractive and accountability is … sexy. If it's hard for you to be accountable, start with something small. Apologize for it sincerely. And watch your partner's shocked expression.

Wednesday--Stop dissing your partner to your friends. You may feel that you're detoxifying by sharing the latest horrors with your posse, but you're actually poisoning your own attitude with each drop of disrespect you spread. Your complaints may all be valid, but they belong in a therapist or counselor's office, where they can be examined objectively and discussed with your partner in a context of healing. It's one thing to seek advice from a friend or confidant about a problem in your relationship. It's another to seek validation of your grievances. The insults you sling when you're away linger on your lips when you come home and permeate the air even if you don't speak them.

Thursday—Stop holding grudges. Yes, I know. There's stuff you just can't let go of, things you can't forgive. I could tell you things my ex said to me (and she has her own flash points), but I won't do that here. But there's a difference between returning to these in every conversation, lording them over your partner, and using them as leverage to get your needs met. Forgiveness means moving past the bump—or even crater—in the road and looking ahead towards the rest of the journey. Forgiveness means keeping your eyes on the prize.

Friday—Stop being the smaller person. If you lower your standard of behavior to your partner's, let's face it, you're sunk. How will things ever improve? It's 'til death do you part, not a fight unto death, so stop doing things or not doing things out of bitterness and spite. Someone has to be the bigger person, to take on a burden when the other refuses. The question is, will that person be you?

Saturday—Stop sniping. Relationships founder over the little things. Tone of voice. Disrespectful comments. Jokes at your partner's expense. No single instance of this stuff amounts to anything, but a constant barrage of negativity will bring the whole thing down after a while. You may feel better after getting your dig in, but you're not making anything better, because what you're really doing is dumping your hurt feelings on your partner while simultaneously saying, you can't help me. If you actually want your partner to engage with what's bothering you, learn to present it in a constructive way.

Sunday—Stop and take stock. On the seventh day, God rested. Relax and spend a few minutes thinking about your week. Ask yourself, and answer honestly. Did the diet make a difference? Do you feel like things are better or worse? Does your interaction with your partner feel less toxic and more ... cleansed? Another week is starting tomorrow. A week can make a world of difference. Why not give it a try?

7 Things I Wish I'd Known Before My Two Crazy Marriages

Wisdom drawn from two dysfunctional relationships that both ended in divorce.

——

I had a sucky first marriage. And a crappy second one, too. Some of it was about my partners. But a lot of it was about me. And all of it was because of me, meaning because of my choices—not just the partners I chose to be with, but how I chose to behave in my relationships, how I chose to respond, what I chose to believe (or deny, or delude myself into believing), the story I chose to fabricate for the world, and the courses of action I pursued—courses that may have been in my self-interest but surely weren't in my best interest—along with my inability to distinguish between the two. That was a long sentence, but I was married for a total of 18 years, so I have a lot to say.

I'm also going to hold my tongue. This post is not an indictment of my ex-wives. It's about taking responsibility for my own contributions, and helping other men and women who have been in, are stuck in, or are trying to exit similar situations get a handle on what's happening and take appropriate action, as well as preventing others who have yet to experience the exquisite torture of a dysfunctional relationship from unnecessary suffering. So here are the seven things I wish I'd known before my two crazy marriages.

◆◇◆

1. My emotional resources are not infinite. As we get older, we acknowledge we aren't going to live forever, but it often takes a lot longer to admit we can't love certain people forever—that we can't soothe every ruffled feather (real or imaginary), absorb every intentional or unintentional blow, tolerate the poison of every toxic outburst, and navigate the floodwaters of constant negativity without our own reserves of love, goodwill, emotional energy, and sanity running dangerously dry. I thought I could do it all, especially given my secure, love-filled childhood, my seemingly endless patience, my people-pleasing skills, and my superior intelligence, which I didn't realize was sorely lacking in its emotional quotient. High SAT scores and an Ivy League degree don't prepare you to deal with dysfunction—your own or someone else's. Compulsive givers always think we can give just a little bit more ... until we realize we can't. And then, we feel like a failure, and we try to keep giving—from emptiness. Giving from emptiness creates that horrible hollowed-out feeling and embodies the phrase, "he's just a shell of his former self." Focus on those words—former self. Because when you reach the end of your emotional rope, the self has been lost, abandoned in the fruitless quest to please another, and that loss has happened in the same way Hemingway describes bankruptcy in The Sun Also Rises: "Gradually, then suddenly."

2. Damage to the psyche is cumulative. This is the devastating corollary to number 1. We feel hurt; we get over it. We feel hurt; we get over it. Early on, the hurt seems bearable with sufficient pauses between injuries, our recovery fast enough, and the possibility that it will stop real. We think we can take it (I did), and we convince ourselves that pain will make us a stronger, better person. But as time passes, our damaged areas, tenderized by relentless assaults, become weeping open wounds that never heal completely. Damage to the psyche is not like a cut or a bruise, or even a broken bone, which can heal satisfactorily with few or no after-effects. Damage to the psyche has a half-life, and the stronger the damage, the longer it remains. Hurt a person at the core, cut him or her to the quick, and every new attack not only aggravates the old wound but precludes it from closing up, knitting together, and sealing over with healthy new skin. And damage to the psyche is also silent. This is why people in dysfunctional relationships reach a tipping point that often surprises both partners. In the movies, you see actors get riddled with bullets but keep on walking as if nothing has happened, then finally fall. You can only walk wounded for so long.

3. Broken people have to want to heal themselves. I was born with a gift for helping hurt people feel better, but I put too much stock in my own power. Healing and being healthy is a choice, and as partners of hurt people, we can only facilitate, not enact their healing. You can't make people take care of themselves, or address their psychological and emotional issues, especially if they don't admit they have any. Even a diagnosis doesn't always set the scene for treatment or a cure. Broken people who devote their energy to breaking others so they can feel better about their brokenness have a lot invested in the lie that there's nothing wrong with them—and that it's all you. Their whole philosophy and world view are at stake, and dissing the diagnoser is much more appealing —and requires less effort—than dealing with the disease. They also find it preferable to use you as their happy drug, while blaming your inadequacies—some of which are real—for their misery. When you care about someone who's broken, it's excruciatingly painful and may even break something inside of you to realize that no matter how much love you pour on their wounds, and no matter how often you suture, you can't heal them, that you can only surrender that healing to their own motivation, modern medicine, and God.

4. Emotional cruelty is never acceptable or excusable —ever. People—and especially intimate partners—get angry. Mostly, we get angry because we care. But there's a huge difference between anger and cruelty. Anger is about expressing your own feelings of hurt, frustration, and indignation, with the goal of getting better treatment. Cruelty is about inflicting hurt on someone else, causing that person to feel pain. Cruel words hurt, but it's the lies we tell ourselves to excuse those words that hurt the most. "He didn't mean it." "She overreacted." "It was the heat of the moment." "She has a temper." And the worst, "I deserved it." No pain, no gain may apply in exercise, but certain kinds of emotional pain don't lead to growth or offer any benefit. On the contrary, this pain shrinks us and causes us to withdraw into ourselves. We begin to believe that our punishment is merited, that our partner "has a right to be angry," and that we don't deserve love. When we accept emotional cruelty, we redefine love as allowing another to violate our boundaries, instead of a willing, conscious choice to open our heart to a respectful person who deserves to inhabit our sacred space. Emotional cruelty is infidelity that occurs within the relationship.

5. If it doesn't feel right, it isn't right. It's really that simple. Let your instincts be your guide. When something's wrong you feel unsettled. Nervous. Nauseated. You tremble and twitch. Your health starts to falter. If it feels forced, you're forcing it, even if that's uncomfortable to admit. In a blog post a while back, I described what I called "Situational Dysfunction."

> *... a feeling of discomfort, a nagging sense that things are not as they should be. Given that many of us probably feel this a lot of the time, it is difficult to attach the feeling to its root cause. Often in dysfunctional relationships we find ourselves doing things that we are not comfortable doing, such as covering for another person's inability to function or hiding—from ourselves as well as others—what is truly happening. What makes this even more difficult for us to understand what is happening is that the discomfort becomes pervasive, constant, and expected, and therefore starts to move from the conscious foreground of our experience to the subconscious background.*

When discomfort becomes embedded in your everyday life, as it did in mine, it starts to feel ... normal. And your understanding of normal becomes reversed. When you accept a dysfunctional relationship, you tolerate continual assaults on the self, and as the self weakens you become less able to trust yourself, less able to assert your needs, embrace your values, and be who you are.

6. Never sacrifice yourself for the sake of the relationship. For this piece of wisdom, I credit my therapist, because I had it wrong. I thought you put the relationship first and kept sacrificing. He helped me learn to put myself first, and that the health of the relationship depends on that choice. When we sacrifice ourselves, we begin to feel resentment, which is the root of martyrdom and self-justification for treating a partner as badly as he or she treats us. If your partner truly loves you, there should be no objection to your protecting, preserving, and defending your self from harm, and from preventing your self from being sacrificed at the feet of another. Recently, Maya Angelou appeared on "Super Soul Sunday" and offered similar guidance in response to Oprah's asking what was the best advice she'd ever given.

> There's a place in you that you must keep inviolate. You must keep it pristine, clean, so that nobody has a right to curse you or treat you badly. Nobody, no mother, father, no wife or husband—nobody. Because that may be the place you go to when you meet God. You have to have a place that you say, "Stop it. Back up. You must not. No. Absolutely." Say no. When it's no, say so.

If you cede the place she is talking about to another, if you allow someone to trample on your sacred ground, you experience a soul-withering combination of loss, bitterness, and regret that renders you unable to be a full partner or even to function as a fully actuated person in the world. Don't do it. Please don't.

7. Making emotionally healthy choices the hardest thing we do. It seems like it should be easy. We try to eat right, exercise, avoid unhealthy habits like smoking or drinking too much. We take all sorts of precautions to protect our physical and financial security. But when it comes to allowing emotionally unhealthy people into our lives, we have an enormous blind spot. There are two reasons. First, unhealthy people meet deep psychological needs. They provide us instant gratification—the intense love and admiration we've dreamed of. They offer constant validation—until we cross them. They present a shiny surface of love and brightness and potential—while engaging in machinations, indoctrination, procrastination, and endless explanation as to why it's all our fault that things aren't working. They'd be better if we only loved them more. And we have a tendency to believe them, especially if we lack confidence or have low self-esteem. Choosing self-interest over best interest, we rationalize getting all the good stuff as a worthwhile tradeoff for occasional pain and intermittent abuse, mixed with equal parts of degradation and disrespect. We treat these things as anomalies and fail to see the pattern. The second reason we end up with unhealthy partners is our failure to acknowledge our own unhealthiness, to see that in choosing someone who harms us, we choose to harm ourselves. Unfortunately, there's no Surgeon General's warning on people, no label that says, "This potential partner is hazardous to your health." But if you take the advice I've given here to heart, you might just spare yourself a lot of heartache.

The 1 Thing Happy People Don't Do

Here's a single, simple pitfall that happy people avoid.

―――

When we are no longer able to change a situation, we are challenged to change ourselves.

―Viktor Frankl, Man's Search for Meaning

―――

And I ain't the Lord, no I'm just a fool
Learning loving somebody don't make them love you

- Jack Johnson, *Sitting, Wishing, Waiting*

―――

A while back I wrote a Facebook status that I knew would turn into an article for **The Good Men Project**.

When we remain in an unhealthy relationship, we believe we are waiting for our partner to change. In truth, we are waiting for ourselves to change, a process that often takes longer than we expect.

It took me 15 years to figure this out―much longer than I expected―and another seven to connect it with happiness, and I believe this fundamental misconception is responsible for millions of unhappy relationships—both personal and professional—and perhaps billions of unhappy people. Yes, billions.

♦◊♦

So here's the nut: **Happy people don't try to change other people or wait for them to change. They work only on themselves.**

It's stunningly simple.

But stunningly difficult to embrace.

Why?

Because we tend to believe that happy people are lucky and unhappy people aren't. It's easier to believe that, more comfortable to believe that, than to admit that happiness is a choice, or more accurately, the result of a series of choices.

Put another way, it's easier to answer the question, "Why am I so unlucky?" than "Why am I so unhappy?" because the second question requires deep introspection and achieving self-awareness, while the first can only be acknowledged as rhetorical or answered with a statement that avoids personal accountability (e.g., "Because God hates me"), because luck by definition is beyond our control.

In *Thinking, Fast and Slow*, Daniel Kahneman's groundbreaking exploration of intuitive and deliberate thinking, he explains the phenomenon of replacing one question with another: "When faced with a difficult question, we often answer an easier one instead, usually without noticing the substitution."

Happy people may appear not to be doing any work to be happy. It just seems to flow for them. But happy people always return the focus to the more difficult question, the one with an answer that in all likelihood requires hard work on the self, while their unhappier counterparts default to the belief—and false sense of relief—that others need to change, a belief that is fatal to their pursuit of peace and contentment. The sooner we learn that people only change when they want to, at their own rate, on their own schedule, the sooner we can get busy on ourselves. Personal growth can be encouraged from without but can only occur from within.

In conjunction with the flawed belief that others must change first, we also put too much faith in our power to influence others, setting ourselves up for crushing disappointment—and potentially paralyzing depression—when we fail in our futile attempts to change them. This often leads to our stepping it up (because we've been trained never to quit and to keep trying harder), and trying to force change through threats and manipulation. Can you think of a greater recipe for unhappiness than that? Except perhaps engaging in an endless, pointless struggle?

Happy people are not the shiny, lucky, blessed ones to whom nothing bad ever seems to happen. They're the ones who handle the bad stuff in stride.

And it's not that happy people don't have losses. They do, just like the rest of us. But they act faster to cut them and move on.

So the next time you're wondering, ask yourself, "Where am I focusing my change energy? On others? Or on myself?"

The answer will tell you everything you need to know about being happy.

5 Keys to Emotional Independence

Too often we give others the power to make us happy or sad. These five powerful keys help you take your emotional life back.

———

One summer a number of years ago, I was riding the commuter train into New York, and an attractive young woman sat down next to me. Dark hair, green eyes, slender build, engaging smile. She was quite forward and wasted no time starting a conversation. She also let me know immediately how smart she was. I quickly learned she was a freshman at a prestigious Ivy League university with a coveted summer internship at a prestigious foundation. She then turned to the topic of her boyfriend, who was a year younger and had just finished high school, and who had the nerve to start dating another girl when my seat mate went off to college. She and the boyfriend were still "more than best friends," and this bright, beautiful girl was trying to accept the idea that she would be one of two women in his dating life. She lamented, "If he would only decide that he really wants to be with me, I would be so happy." I turned and said to her, "Why on earth are you giving him that power?" I asked her what she wanted and told her that if her so-called boyfriend couldn't give it to her, she should go find it somewhere else. I explained they don't teach these things in college. She was astonished.

Most of us fundamentally misunderstand emotional independence. We think it means not needing anyone or being alone. Emotional independence is nothing more than the power to make choices and the integrity to align those choices with our needs. We can choose the peace and simplicity of solitude, or we can embrace the excitement of intimacy and the complexity of long-term companionship. Either way, we must understand these are choices we make, not choices that have been made for us. Mastering the five keys to emotional independence not only frees you to make personal choices that serve you but also enables you to close the door on pathways— and people—who don't.

1. You are responsible for your own emotions. This means you—and not another person's words, actions, beliefs, or lack thereof—are responsible for how you feel at any given moment. A person may say or do something hurtful, your partner may cheat on you or badmouth you to a friend, but the feelings of hurt, disappointment, anger and whatever else constitutes your reaction—these originate, exist in, and belong to you. Think about how you take care of a house or car you own as opposed to one you lease or rent, and apply this attitudinal shift to your feelings. You'll start taking care of yourself—and others—differently.

2. You are responsible for managing your own emotions. This sounds so similar to the first point that you may ask, why bother? But the distinction is crucial. Because the emotions you feel originate in you, it is up to you to deal with them and formulate a mature, healthy, and effective response—as opposed to simply reacting. In addition, if you consistently experience unhealthy emotions that influence your actions, it is up to you and you alone to manage your moods to minimize their destructive impact on the people you love. Abusers are people who lack emotional control and won't own the need to get help. Instead, they say their partners made them do it. Making your partner or anyone else your emotional caretaker, using another person as a punching bag for your self-loathing or as medicine for your illness, creates a dangerous co-dependency and a toxic dynamic that will eventually destroy your relationship.

3. You are never responsible for another person's emotions or for managing their moods. This is the logical flip side of points 1. and 2. It doesn't stop you from being sympathetic, empathetic, and compassionate when someone you care about is hurting. You can minister to people in distress, try to soothe their pain, and help them heal. But ultimately, any treatment you apply is topical, for external use only; it may alleviate the symptoms, but it won't cure the disease, and your help is a gift and not an obligation. Even if you help someone change they way he or she feels about something, remember you didn't change the person—you only helped that person learn how to change themselves. Real, lasting change only comes from inside.

4. Never, ever take the bait. People who don't practice 1. and 2. and don't accept 3. will try their hardest to make you responsible for how they feel and what they do, especially when those feelings and actions hurt you. This is the heart of relationship dysfunction. Remember point 3. You're not responsible. Obviously this doesn't absolve you or give you carte blanche to enrage or hurt others. But it does free you from the suffocating stranglehold an emotionally unhealthy person can place on your psyche, and it enables you to walk away from situations orchestrated to draw you in, induce a predictable reaction, start a fight, and pull you down to the other person's level. Keep your head above water, and don't take the bait.

5. Practice consistency. Emerson called it the hobgoblin of small minds, but consistency is the fifth and most critical key to achieving and maintaining emotional independence. You may fall short at times, fall back into old habits, get caught up or drawn into someone else's drama because it suits your own momentary needs, and begin to feel responsible for another actor's lines. We all do. When this happens, remember that you're the author, producer, and director of your own play. You set the stage. You cast the characters. You choose the part you want. You operate the lights and curtain. And you get to take the bow. It's your show and no one else's.

I don't know what the young woman decided or how her life ended up. I never saw her again on the train, and she's not my responsibility. But I do hope I taught her something. And I hope she declared her emotional independence.

5 Words That Will Change Your Life

A five-word epiphany on finding happiness and fulfillment.

———

You've got to know when to hold 'em
Know when to fold 'em
Know when to walk away
And know when to run

\- Kenny Rogers, *The Gambler*

———

I know. The headline reads like clickbait. But I promise you this, and I don't promise lightly: The five words you are about to read hold the power to change your life—that is, if you choose to let them. I know, because they changed mine.

Only stay where you're valued.

◆◇◆

These words express a simple premise, but one that is perhaps the most difficult to adhere to, and especially hard for anyone who—as a child or adult—has been made to feel broken and unworthy. The challenge of following this rule is twofold: first to recognize devaluing relationships—at work, in friendships, at home, even with ourselves; and second to summon the courage to leave.

Only stay where you're valued.

What are the signs of a devaluing relationship? They can be obvious or subtle and insidious. If your partner, friend, or boss talks down to you, insults you, bullies or intimidates you, and otherwise treats you like a worthless piece of crap, it's clear you're being devalued, though you may try to deny it because it doesn't align with your sense of who you are. It's harder to see devaluing behavior when you're under-appreciated, undermined, unsupported, and taken for granted by someone who signs your paycheck or treats you like one. Being devalued is often less about what's being done to you than about what's left undone or withheld, the absent gratitude, the praise that's never spoken, and we often get used to living on scraps, awaiting a feast that will never be served.

Only stay where you're valued.

Being employed does not mean you're valued.

Being in a relationship does not mean you're valued.

Being financially supported does not mean you're valued.

Being taken care of does not mean you're valued.

Being made love to does not mean you're valued.

Being told you're beautiful does not mean you're valued.

Being put on a pedestal does not mean you're valued.

Being called on for every crisis does not mean you're valued.

Being told you are loved does not mean you're valued.

Being loved for what you give and not for who you are does not mean you're valued.

Only stay where you're valued.

Learn to distinguish being used from being valued.

When you feel depleted, diminished, and discouraged, you're being used.

When you feel enriched, empowered, and encouraged, you're valued.

When your contributions are unseen, unmentioned, and unrewarded, you're being used.

When your contributions are acknowledged, appreciated, and advertised, you're valued.

Listen quietly to your heart, and you'll know if you're valued.

Only stay where you're valued.

Our sense of self-worth does not depend on the estimation of others. We are all worthy. But our feelings of happiness and contentment center on knowing intellectually and feeling on a deep emotional level that we matter, that our life brings value to other people.

Only stay where you're valued.

When you spend time in a devaluing relationship, you become convinced that no one will value you. This makes it difficult to walk away. You think things can only get worse, that the devaluing situation is the best you can do —and the best you deserve. Walking away takes strength, belief in yourself, resolve to move forward, and the courage to take a risk. It also requires the awareness that the risk of being continually reduced is nothing less than personal evaporation.

When you walk away, you might be alone for a while. But the odds are good you'll find something better. And to that I say, "Deal me in."

Conclusion

The really simple bottom line is that you get to decide what kind of intimate relationship you have. You're in charge, whether you're aware of it or not. Blaming your partner for all your relationship problems is a form of avoidance; you're denying your own contribution to the dysfunctional dynamic. Your contribution may be as basic as tolerating and enabling hurtful behavior from your partner, which doesn't ever mean you're causing hurt or abuse but does mean you're not setting boundaries and taking effective action to stop it. Or you may be a bigger player in the game. The articles here are intended to help you identify the dysfunctional dynamic, come to see your own role in it, carefully examine your reasons for staying —because there are always reasons—and make a conscious, informed, independent decision on how you want to move forward. So many of us cling to unhappy situations because they're familiar, because we're afraid leaving will be worse, because we lie to ourselves about the silver lining, or because we hang on desperately to those brief glimmers of joy that seem to give hope to an otherwise dark existence.

With the perspective I've provided, you can educate yourself and take control of your situation, take back your power as an equal, and decide to do what's right for you. Staying and working to improve a dysfunctional relationship may be what you want, and if that's your choice, at least now you're choosing, instead of being sucked into something you don't understand. Or leaving may be your best option. If you do decide to go and are feeling guilty about leaving your partner, remember these words: **Getting out is not giving up on someone when staying is giving up on yourself**. Good luck!

Photo Credits

The 7 Deadly Signs of a Dysfunctional Relationship: Wikimedia Commons

The Silent Pain of Emotional Withholding: Wikimedia Commons

21 Signs Your Relationship Is Doomed: Guian Bolisay/ Flickr

5 Signs You're Being Played by a 'Victim': Alyssa L. Miller/ Flickr

This Guy Makes Your Abuser Look Good: macnolete/ Flickr

5 Lies That Keep Us Stuck in Dysfunctional Relationships:

Top photo—Peter/Flickr

Middle photo—Neil Moralee/Flickr

Bottom photo—john_worsley_uk/Flickr

The 3 Big Lies Abusers Rely On: Michiel Jelijs/Flickr

Why We Stay With People Who Hurt Us: Dustin Gaffke/ Flickr

7 Ugly Reasons We Cling When We Should Leave: Nate Steiner/Flickr

Why Couples Fight: The Real Cause of Conflict: tambakothejaguar/Flickr

A Theory on the Role of Love in Abuse: Eliza/Flickr

When Leaving Seems Impossible …: Kate Ter Haar/Flickr

5 Reasons It's So Hard to Leave Crazy: Loren Javier/Flickr

The 7-Day Relationship Detox Diet: Joanna Slodownik/Flickr

7 Things I Wish I'd Known Before My Two Crazy Marriages: Daniel Oines/Flickr

The 1 Thing Happy People Don't Do: Nathan O'Nions/Flickr

5 Keys to Emotional Independence: Photo courtesy of author

Conclusion: DieselDemon/Flickr

Thomas G. Fiffer's other books, including *What Is Love? A Guide for the Perplexed to Matters of the Heart,* are available on Amazon. You can also find him on **The Good Men Project**.

Made in the USA
San Bernardino, CA
02 October 2017